What the critics are saying...

"...will have you shivering and burning all at the same time." ~ *Romance Reviews Today*

"...heated moments tipping the scorcher scale." ~ *Karen Find Out About New Books*

5 Roses "Ms. Taylor`s off-beat comedy made me laugh until the tears flowed. This unique, naughty novel has won a lifetime fan in me." ~ *A Romance Review*

TAWNY TAYLOR

BODY AND Soul

ELLORA'S CAVE
ROMANTICA PUBLISHING

An Ellora's Cave Romantica Publication

www.ellorascave.com

Body and Soul

ISBN # 1419953559
ALL RIGHTS RESERVED.
Pesky Paranormals Copyright© 2005 Tawny Taylor
Phantasmic Fantasies Copyright © 2005 Tawny Taylor
Edited by Sue-Ellen Gower
Cover art by Syneca

Electronic book Publication July 2005
Trade paperback Publication February 2006

Excerpt from *Wet and Wilde* Copyright © 2004 Tawny Taylor

Warning:

The following material contains graphic sexual content meant for mature readers. *Body and Soul* has been rated *E-rotic* by a minimum of three independent reviewers.

Ellora's Cave Publishing offers three levels of Romantica™ reading entertainment: S (S-ensuous), E (E-rotic), and X (X-treme).

S-*ensuous* love scenes are explicit and leave nothing to the imagination.

E-*rotic* love scenes are explicit, leave nothing to the imagination, and are high in volume per the overall word count. In addition, some E-rated titles might contain fantasy material that some readers find objectionable, such as bondage, submission, same sex encounters, forced seductions, etc. E-rated titles are the most graphic titles we carry; it is common, for instance, for an author to use words such as "fucking", "cock", "pussy", etc., within their work of literature.

X-*treme* titles differ from E-rated titles only in plot premise and storyline execution. Unlike E-rated titles, stories designated with the letter X tend to contain controversial subject matter not for the faint of heart.

Also by Tawny Taylor

ɛɔ

~ Contents ~

Pesky Paranormals

ઝ

Trademarks Acknowledgement

~

Prologue

ဆ

This story isn't for people who won't believe in what they can't see. It's a strange tale and I admit if it hadn't happened to me, I never would've believed such a crazy, improbable thing was possible. Yes, a long, long time ago, I too was a logical but close-minded person who only believed in what could be seen, touched, smelled, tasted or heard.

All that changed very suddenly one day.

Sometimes truth is stranger than fiction…thank God. Because in the end, I am quite pleased with the results. But I'm getting ahead of myself. Better get back to the beginning.

My name is Stephanie Burbank and this is my incredible story—believe it or not. As it unfolds, I challenge you to open your mind and question what you've believed since learning Santa Claus was your dad, the Easter bunny your mom, and ghosts, fairies and superheroes only existed in your imagination.

After all—to bastardize a famous expression—truth is in the eye of the beholder.

Read on, if you dare…

Chapter One

❧

The day *he* died, Stephanie Burbank thought she'd be rid of him forever. She learned rather quickly she couldn't have been more wrong.

He was her pain-in-the-ass, control-freak ex-husband. It seemed that even after being the victim of a motor vehicle-versus-pedestrian fatal accident—a terrible trauma to say the least—he couldn't let her go. In fact, he was more of a pain in the ass, control-freak dead than he ever dreamed of being alive.

Who would've thought?

Considering his history, she should have guessed. But formerly lacking any faith in the afterlife, she found believing in ghosts wasn't exactly easy...at least not the first few months. After that, she became surprisingly comfortable with their unique relationship—marked by the unmistakable sounds he would make during even her most private times.

The man had no couth.

To make matters worse, recently he had acquired some new skills, adopted some methods that were seriously cramping her social life. And sex? Forget about it! Wasn't happening. Not when every time she got down to her skivvies with a prospective hunk *he* would make something crazy happen to ruin the mood, like catch the poor guy's shorts on fire.

It seemed there was no escaping it. She'd recently started calling it "The Ex Curse". After visits to psychics, the local priest, a couple shrinks and at least a half-dozen miserable dates that ended with her delivering the poor guy to the emergency room, she finally accepted the fact that, dead or alive, ex-husband Jeremy Burbank was going to make sure her life was a living hell...for eternity.

But just because she'd resigned herself to that fact didn't mean she wasn't frustrated, and that irritation intensified when Rafe Hammond moved into the condo next door.

Rafe wasn't your average run-of-the-mill working stiff. He was a god in Dockers and a golf shirt. His jet-black hair was just messy enough to be sexy, his smile usually a little off-kilter and his body...there were no words for what lay hidden below the sharp-creased cotton trousers and shirts boasting his membership to one of southeast Michigan's finest country clubs. Well-developed muscles covered every inch of his frame—she'd seen practically everything last summer at the pool when, gaping like an ass, she'd nearly drowned after tripping over a chair and falling in the deep end.

She couldn't swim to save her life.

That was the single time in the past year and a half that a man who had touched her had not instantaneously combusted. Evidently even an arsonist ghost couldn't set someone under twelve feet of water on fire. That could be the only reason why he hadn't scorched like the rest of them, either that or Jeremy wasn't ready to let her out of her misery yet. She figured even he couldn't be cruel enough to watch her drown to death, her fault or not.

Still, armed with the knowledge that even a kiss could land her hunkilicious neighbor in the burn ward, she didn't dare pursue anything more intimate than a casual neighborly friendship with him. On a daily basis, they exchanged small talk, every now and then a cup of milk or a power tool.

Until today.

This morning—a Saturday, her favorite day of the week—she'd woken up after a restless night, in the mood to give Jeremy hell. He hadn't let her get five minutes of sleep, filling her room with the most God-awful banging until daybreak. What had she done to deserve this?

Anyway, if there was one thing that highlighted the less noble aspects of her personality, it was lack of sleep. Lack of chocolate came in a close second.

Grumbling to Jeremy about the satisfaction of revenge when she found it, she walked outside to get her mail and her mood lifted instantly.

"Hey," Rafe said, wearing his usual lopsided grin and a pair of low-slung boxers with hearts. He looked fresh out of bed, rumpled and sleepy, exactly the way she liked him.

"Morning." Too busy checking out his abs—which were picture-perfect if she did say so herself—she dropped her mailbox key, which naturally bounced two times and landed in the tiny crevice between the brick wall and the concrete porch. "Oh, shoot!" Kneeling down, she dug at it with her fingernails, ruining her manicure. "Why do these things always happen to me?"

He stooped next to her, caught her hands in his and gave her a smile that could easily have caused her to combust. "Please. Allow me."

Her mind racing ahead as she visualized a few dozen things she'd gladly allow him do, she forced herself to look down at the concrete. "It's stuck pretty good."

"I've dropped mine in there before. If you take a magnetized screwdriver—which I just happen to carry every time I come out here because you never know when it'll come in handy—you can get it out of there lickety-split. He pulled a slot-head screwdriver out of the waist of his boxer shorts—that couldn't be a very safe place to keep that—and shoved the narrow head into the gap. A second later, he handed her the key.

When their fingers touched, little jolts of electricity buzzed up her arm. She sat there frozen, stunned as at least a couple of hundred watts of pure, unadulterated lust charged through her system.

He didn't move either.

Then it dawned on her. So far, he hadn't burst into flame. That was twice now. This man had touched her two times and hadn't been burned. Had she found someone Jeremy couldn't hurt for some reason?

Her mind raced with the possibilities—and there were quite a few. But the one she most enjoyed entertaining was the thought that she could fuck this gorgeous guy to her heart's content and Jeremy couldn't do a thing to stop her. Was it possible? Could it be? If so, there was a God!

Willing to risk getting singed around the edges, she licked her lips and leaned forward. Surely a kiss would tell.

And it told…a lot of things.

As her mouth touched his, her whole body came alive. Her heart rate at least doubled and both shivers and heat waves coursed through her body. It was instant chemistry, the kind she hadn't felt before with anyone. Not even Jeremy.

Rafe seemed to be enjoying it too. His quickened breathing melded with hers as she opened her mouth. His tongue slipped inside and performed a sexy little tango with hers, and the only flames she sensed were the mini-blazes igniting in her panties.

A round of the Hallelujah Chorus sang in her head...until something ice-cold landed on it. The initial freeze was followed by a second torrent of icy liquid.

Any heat she had felt instantly extinguished, she gasped as the cold substance ran down her body. Still trying to catch her breath, she jumped to her feet. Her gaze lifted heavenward as she searched for the source but found nothing but a clear blue sky and two rows of closed windows.

Had Jeremy discovered a new weapon?

She pushed her sopping hair out of her eyes and shouted, "Jeremy, if that was you, it wasn't funny."

"Who's Jeremy?" Rafe asked.

Without thinking, she wrapped her arms around herself and responded, "My good-for-nothing ex husband." She caught him staring at her chest and glanced down.

Egads! She was indecent. Thanks to the unexpected cold shower, her white T-shirt was not only translucent but also clinging to her boobs. She was wearing no bra and her nipples resembled little pink pebbles poking stiffly at the fabric. If she were on Spring Break in Fort Lauderdale, she'd be a hit.

Unfortunately, or fortunately depending upon how one looked at it, she was in Michigan. And Spring Break was several months in the past. In an attempt to maintain a small amount of dignity, she inched her crossed arms higher over her chest to hide her nipples. "Gotta go. Sorry about that." She made a hasty dash for her front door but a quick yank on the waist of her soggy T-shirt stopped her in her tracks.

* * * * *

This wasn't happening. Not again! Rafe silently cursed the night he'd paid a visit to the crackpot who called herself a spiritual guide and gone home with a castaway ghost who amused herself by soaking every female who came within twenty feet of him with ice water. He caught the edge of his neighbor's wet T-shirt and gave it another yank.

"Are you okay?" Damn that little spirit! Thanks to her, he hadn't been able to get any nookie in almost three months! He'd get the better of her someday, soon as he figured out how.

Stephanie turned slowly, mumbling words he could barely make out and pointing up at the windows, "I need to go... Jeremy has a terrible sense of humor... I'm so sorry... I swear, someday..."

Who was Jeremy? Their condo building was a duplex. He knew he wasn't living with a guy named Jeremy.

"...my ex-husband..."

What had she said about an ex-husband? He glanced up again.

She was living with her ex-husband? If so, why was she making the moves on him, in plain daylight, for all to see? And why would he throw water on their heads? What the hell was going on? Was this a joke?

Were they swingers, maybe? Newly converted swingers? Not once since he'd moved in had she ever acted like this before.

Well, there had been that time when she'd groped him in the swimming pool. He had always assumed her grabbing him *there* had been an accident. After all, she'd nearly drowned.

Didn't drowning people grab things in their panic?

Not a guy's cock, you idiot!

Had he been missing an opportunity all this time?

Well, now, after a more obvious sign—that kiss couldn't have been an accident—he was not about to let her mumble some incoherent apology and run off! A guy could only take so much.

Hoping Annabelle wouldn't send more buckets of ice water cascading from the sky, he pulled her closer. "What are you talking about? Do you live with your ex-husband? I've never seen him."

Stephanie blanched, giving him the impression she wasn't about to tell him the truth. "No."

"Then how could he get up there to dump the water?"

"It's a long story and a little bit complicated."

"Well, after that kiss, don't you think you owe me an explanation?"

She staggered backward, threatening to trip over the pot of weedy flowers on the porch stoop and he grabbed her arms to help steady her.

She seemed to get her feet back under her but the contact between his hands and her skin, and resulting heat rising from his nether regions, was making him a little unsteady too. He wrapped his arms around her waist to support them both.

Not a good idea. They were bathed in water again.

He shook his head like a dog and looked down at her, hoping she wouldn't get hysterical like all the other women had. Most women didn't care to have their expensive clothes and hairdos ruined, even if it was just water.

At least she'd been wearing pajamas and from the look of it hadn't gotten around to fixing her hair and makeup.

Instead of acting like a girl and getting hysterical like he expected, she laughed and he found himself laughing right along with her as he released her and took one step backward.

Their hair was plastered flat to their heads, hers clinging to her neck, shoulders and chest, partially obscuring his once-clear view of her breasts.

Their clothes were saturated. Water dripped from his chin. He glanced around to see if the neighbors were staring yet. Both wet and shivering and laughing like a couple of crazed idiots, they had to look ridiculous. Someone was bound to call for the men in white coats soon.

At least his drawers had cooled. Strange, it had almost felt like they were burning.

"I'm sorry." Her arms lifted and she ran her long, graceful fingers through her sodden chestnut hair, the motion leaving those twin peaks out there front and center and in clear view where they belonged.

He couldn't help staring. Again. Hey, he was a guy. He could appreciate a set of nice boobs. And she had them, boy did she ever. Had to be at least Cs but he wouldn't ask. That probably wouldn't score him any points on the gentleman scale, not that the ice baths would either. But for some reason, she seemed to think her ex-husband was at fault for those.

"This is really funny. I don't know what to say." Clearly catching on to what he was staring at, she glanced down again and promptly folded her arms over her chest.

He gave himself a mental kick in the ass. Where were his manners? "No, I'm sorry. I can't seem to help looking... I mean, they're...er..." *Shit! I sound like an ass.* "...you're very beautiful."

The slight blue hue around her lips faded as her face tinted a sexy shade of pink. It was a nice change. He wondered how far down her chest it extended. "That water was cold," she stuttered.

"Yes, it was."

"I better get inside before another bucketful falls on my head. I'm bound to come down with pneumonia." She didn't move.

"In that case, you'd better hustle inside," he agreed. He gathered his forgotten mail, which was as soggy as the rest of his things and followed her to their front doors, which stood within inches of each other.

She twisted her doorknob and pushed it open, smiling shyly over her shoulder. "Thanks for the invigorating... chat. This is one Saturday morning I won't soon forget."

"Then how about making it a memorable Saturday afternoon and evening too?" he asked, before he had the chance to chicken out.

"And risk pneumonia?"

"Your ex-husband can't be everywhere. There must be a safe place we can go."

"You'd be surprised."

"Then maybe it's time to go to the police. Stalking's against the law. Unless you're one of those women who like having an ex hang around. I've never understood that but I wouldn't judge you—"

"Believe me, I'm not happy to have him around. He's like a fungus. I can't get rid of him. And if the police could help, I'd have gone there months ago."

Disappointed by her lack of enthusiasm but not surprised, considering the water and the ex-husband thing, he simply nodded. "All right then. I guess we should just call this morning an experiment and go back to being friendly neighbors?"

"I suppose that's best. I'm very sorry. I was hoping…"

"Yeah. Me too."

Ready to give Annabelle hell for the water, he opened his door and stepped into his condo.

Chapter Two

ഉ

Stephanie slammed the front door and yelled into the air, "Jeremy, I see you've learned a new trick, you bastard! Why won't you just leave me alone?"

Frustrated by the fact that she couldn't smack him, she spun around in the air throwing her fists into every inch of space she could reach. Just once, she wished she could do some serious damage. This wasn't fair. "Where the hell are you, you little weasel? God, I want to smack you silly. Why don't you speak to me? Huh? Why stay silent and just do stupid things like set people's clothing on fire and dump water on their heads?"

Then a thought dawned on her.

That made no sense whatsoever. Water and fire didn't mix. Why would he set a fire only to snuff it out with a crapload of ice water?

Unless someone or something else was to blame.

If Jeremy hadn't been at fault, where did the water come from?

"I'm thinking I might be able to get around you, my not-so-pleasant friend," she said aloud as the gears in her head started spinning. "It seems someone else is looking out for Rafe's shorts and I'm willing to test my theory." She tried to think of a place with lots of water for a first date.

A Jacuzzi! Nothing could be better. At least the water would be warm. She knew the perfect place. It would be private, romantic.

She dashed outside and knocked on his front door. The second he opened the door, she said, "You're on. The Bubbly Tub on Main. One o'clock. Wear your bathing suit." When he didn't object, she took that as a yes and ran back into her house to make preparations.

She shaved every part of her body smooth and donned her sexiest bikini and waterproof makeup.

"I'm gonna get lucky today!" she proclaimed as she stuffed a handful of rubbers into her gym bag and shimmied into a pair of loose jogging pants and a jacket. She packed a towel, a few snacks, a bottle of wine and a couple of glasses then drove the couple of miles to their meeting place—one of those tanning and tub places where they rented the tubs by the hour. Her step lively, she half-walked, half-skipped inside. The glasses and wine bottle rattled in her bag.

Rafe was waiting for her in the lobby and did he ever look scrumptious. His swim trunks were a little bulky for her taste but she figured they wouldn't stay on for long anyway. Above the waist, he wore a jogging jacket over a snug T-shirt that gave a hint of the perfect pecs hidden underneath. His hair was back to its usual slightly mussed state, which she found adorable. And his crooked, slightly wicked grin was firmly in place.

Oh yeah. Today would be a day to remember.

"I wasn't sure you'd show up," he said. "Thought maybe it was a joke."

"Oh, no. I wasn't joking."

His gaze raked over her body and she squirmed with pleasure. "I see that now. But before we go inside, I want to tell you I don't think it was your ex-husband who threw the water."

Now that was a shocker. "Then who?"

"It's a long story."

"You'll have plenty of time to tell me later. We have all afternoon if you like," she offered, although talking was the last thing she had in mind. She was determined to make every minute count.

He paid for the Paradise Room, a cozy suite complete with changing area, stall shower and hot tub, then held the door for her. "Shall we?"

"I don't know why I didn't think of this sooner." After stepping inside, she set her bag on the changing area counter and unzipped her jacket. The room was steamy, like a jungle, which suited the décor perfectly. Hordes of tropical plants lined all four walls around the central sunken tub. The walls themselves were covered with one of those real-looking photographic murals. All in all, the room had a very sensual but tranquil feeling. Perfect for what she had in mind. "So what's the story about the water?"

He didn't answer right away. Instead, he took off the jacket and T-shirt, baring his entire upper body.

Holy smoke!

Maybe she could ask about the water later. Considering how long she'd waited for unimpeded sex, the last thing she wanted to do at the moment was chitchat about an insignificant detail. Who cared, as long as it kept him from having his drawers burned? Let the water flow!

She swallowed an enthusiastic shout of approval and maintained some dignity. She kept one eye on his shorts, looking for smoke or flames, as she hungrily drank in the sight of his sun-kissed torso. My goodness, the Mother Sun loved him. There wasn't an inch of his shoulders, arms, stomach or back that wasn't the color of chocolate milk. His smooth-skinned chest rivaled those she'd seen in magazines and his shoulders were the perfect breadth to lean upon. She figured his upper arms had to be about the same circumference as her thighs.

"Just curious. How many hours a day do you spend in the gym?" She felt a bit of drool trying to dribble from the corner of her mouth and swallowed.

"A couple, three or four nights a week. I used to spend more time, practically every night, but I've backed away a bit. Want to live a more balanced life, you know?" He lifted a foot, propping it on a bench, and bent over to untie his shoe, giving her a perfect shot of his rear end.

Would he mind if she bit it?

She bit her lip instead. "Balanced is good."

"That's the way I think too. A little bit of everything, in moderation. That's the way to live."

"I couldn't agree more." Would he think sex twice a night, moderation? Or maybe three times? Surely any more than that would be beyond moderation, wouldn't it?

She took off her jacket and hung it on the hook on the wall then sat on the bench to take off her shoes.

He switched to the other foot, resting it next to her thigh on the bench. His gaze traveled lazily, taking its sweet time, over her face, chest and bare stomach. "You look pretty fit yourself. Do you work out?"

"Not unless you count running after the mailman or sprinting to the shortest checkout line at the grocery store."

"If it keeps you looking like that, it counts." He pulled off his shoe, balled his sock and stuffed it inside, then stood.

Sitting where she was, eye level to his groin, it was easy to see exactly how much he appreciated the subject of their conversation. A noticeable bulge had formed in the front of his drawers.

Things were looking promising indeed!

Unfortunately, he moved beyond reach before she could do anything about it.

She quickly pulled off her jogging pants and hung them on the wall hook with the jacket. As she turned to face him, she sucked in a breath and pushed out her chest to make her stomach look nice and flat and her boobs look bigger.

His hungry expression suggested her effort had created exactly the effect she had been shooting for.

"Wine?" she asked, still holding her breath.

"Sure. I brought some. It's in my bag."

"Me too. What'd you bring?" She rummaged through her stuff, digging to the bottom where the bottle had sunk. Finally feeling it, she lifted it out.

"I brought this Shiraz," he said. "It was recommended by…"

"Wine Spectator dot com?" she finished for him as she read the label on his bottle. "We brought the same wine. How ironic."

"At least we know we share the same taste in wines." He reached into his bag, produced a corkscrew and began the process of opening his bottle.

More content to watch his biceps bunch and flex as he twisted the corkscrew, she blindly rummaged for her glasses and set them on the bench. "And homes," she pointed out. "We share the same taste in homes."

He nodded, pushed the two side arms of the corkscrew down and gave the handle a tug. "Very true. I hadn't thought about that." The cork slid free of the bottle with a delightful *pop*. He poured some wine into both glasses, set the bottle down and after handing a glass to her, lifted his. "A toast?"

"Sure."

"How about to neighbors?"

"To neighbors." She touched her glass to his then lifted it to her mouth, forcing herself to sip daintily rather than succumb to the temptation to gulp. She was nervous as heck. A little wine was always a good cure for the jitters. And this wine was extraordinary, delightful, fruity and sweet, smooth, just the way she liked it. Half a glass went down easy.

Thankfully, she didn't drink often, so that small amount was like liquid courage. She felt alive...and eager to explore the hidden parts of her neighbor's anatomy. She walked to the hot tub and sat on the deck to put her feet into the water.

He sat next to her, his arm grazing her shoulder. "How's the wine?"

Her body registering a strange mix of hot and cold, she shivered. She realized her feet stung and lifted them out of the water. "Delicious. Water's a little too hot though."

"Not a problem. We can turn down the thermostat." He stood to find the controls, but seeing the ribbon of smoldering smoke, Jeremy's doing no doubt, coming from the back of his shorts, she caught his wrist and gave it a firm yank. Caught completely off guard, he toppled into the tub and landed with a huge splash. "What was that for?" he challenged as he stood up, shook his head and sent sparkling droplets of water flying through the air.

She feigned shock. "Oh my gosh! I'm sorry. I didn't mean to do that. I just wanted to get your attention to let you know..." The rest of the sentence kind of got lost somewhere between her head and her mouth.

He was looking at her with the fiercest expression imaginable. It gave her shivers—the good kind. Without speaking a word, he scooped her into his amazing arms, her side pressed against his equally amazing chest...and dropped her into the water.

The sound of churning, thrashing water blasted her ears as she sunk to the bottom. And as she stood, that not-quite-pleasant sound was replaced by a much better one— the sound of his chuckles.

She lunged forward and tried to knock him over but failed miserably. It felt like she'd run smack-dab into a brick wall. He was totally immobile.

Unable to see clearly, thanks to her hair hanging in long, wavy clumps over her face, she gave up on the direct approach, fell back onto the submerged seat, tipped her head back and smoothed her hair away from her face.

He stood before her, waist-deep in the churning, frothy water and folded his arms across his chest. "Truce?"

"Truce." *For now.* Suddenly very thirsty, she reached for her wine glass and polished off the rest.

What a combination! Delicious wine, bubbles and a hot man.

She eyed his mostly full glass and felt guilty for downing hers so quickly. She'd never out-drunk a man before. "Don't you want yours?"

"Not right now."

"How about a snack?"

He nodded. "I'm hungry." Her gaze locked to his tongue as it darted out to moisten his lips. "But not for food."

Those four words were enough to make her shiver with delight. And his expression—fierce man on the hunt—was enough to make her pussy tingle with expectation.

Considering the fire she saw burning in his eyes, he moved much slower than she would have thought as he dropped in front of her and lowered his bulk over top of her chest. Eager to have every inch of his body pressed against hers, she opened her legs to let his hips settle between them. This was heaven! His chest grazed her nipples through the thin material of her bikini and she felt them harden. He tipped his head and nibbled on her neck, his tongue and teeth producing goose bumps over her arms and shoulders.

She instinctively started rocking her hips, pressing her pussy against the thick, hard rod housed in those baggy nylon swim trunks.

He gave a low growl and slid his hands up her legs and around her hips until they were snugly wedged under her bottom. Then he lifted her, sat back and lowered her on top of him. "You have no idea what you're in for," he grumbled.

"Neither do you."

His mouth pressed against hers in a fevered kiss full of urgency and heat. His tongue traced the seam of her mouth and she opened to him. This time, it did more than a tango. It plunged in and out, writhed around, dipping and tasting every bit of her in a wild, untamed dance. Her body stiffened, her legs opened wider, her pussy grated against his cock.

She was on fire, figuratively, and all she could think of was getting those shorts off and impaling herself on that glorious rod.

He lifted his hands and unhooked her bikini top. It fell down to her waist, exposing her breasts, and he wasted no time feasting first on one, pulling the nipple into his mouth and suckling, and then the other. Her head filled with their combined moans and groans of pleasure.

More. She wanted more. She wanted it all.

Standing, she pulled her bikini bottom down and tossed it aside then reached into the foamy froth to find the drawstring to his shorts. Her fingers traced the line of his cock and she heard him suck in a sharp breath.

He caught her wrists before she could do anything else and lifted them out of the water. "Not yet."

"What are you waiting for? Don't you want to?"

"Oh believe me, I want to. I just want to make sure you want to do what I want to, if you know what I mean. I'm not convinced I know how to read you yet, not after this morning. And if we go any further I can't be held responsible for what happens next."

"Okay, read this. Hell yes."

"That's all I needed." He tipped his hips, slid off his shorts, balled them up and lobbed them into the eight-foot banana tree in the corner. The he grabbed her waist and pulled sharply. His erect cock, submerged in bubbles, pressed at her labia.

"What about a rubber?" she asked, hesitating before impaling herself and taking what she hungered for so badly. Head to toe she was stiff and shaking. Tension coiled tight in her belly as excitement and expectation sent wave after wave of giddy heat through her body. "Do they work under water?"

"I hope so. Problem is, they're over there." He pointed toward the banana tree with the shorts dangling from the top.

"I have some." She reluctantly pried herself free from his tight grip, no easy task and not a particularly enjoyable one, and climbed out of the tub to retrieve the rubbers she'd stashed in her bag. Praying she wouldn't look too hopeful, she took the whole strip with her when she returned to the tub.

Better to have them handy than to have to make another dash to the bag later.

He laughed and motioned toward the line of rubbers dangling from her fist. "Have big plans for me, I see."

"A girl's gotta be prepared. As it turns out, it was a good thing I brought these or you'd be climbing that tree over there in the nude. I can't imagine that would feel too good."

"No, probably not." He reached backward and pushed himself up and out of the water and it was only then that she caught her first glimpse of what had been formerly hidden from view.

Holy shit! She should have bought the king-size. She couldn't help staring. Was it real?

Suddenly aware of her gaping mouth, she shut it.

"Weren't prepared for that, were ya?"

"Not exactly." She glanced down at her hand. "Er, I hope "one size fits all". When it comes to women's fashion it sure doesn't."

"They should be fine." He crooked a finger at her and lowered his eyebrows. "Come on over here and let's check."

Her feet felt like cement blocks as she trudged slowly toward him. A whole lot of excitement and a little bit of dread were a powerful elixir, producing some very interesting and unsettling results. Her knees felt wobbly, her heart was beating way too fast for comfort and her head was a little foggy.

Forget about the rubbers. Would that fit in *there*? She'd never had anyone that big before. And it had been so long since she'd had sex. Hadn't she read that pussies shrink from lack of use? Would it feel like she was a virgin all over again?

"Maybe it would be better if we did this out of the water," she offered, figuring she'd need every bit of lubricant that rubber had on it. The water would wash it all away otherwise. At least Jeremy couldn't start the poor guy's shorts on fire now. Not only were they all the way over there, but they were also sopping wet.

"I'm game. Wherever you like is fine with me."

Feeling both excited and a little shy and awkward, she glanced nervously around the room. It wasn't exactly made for fucking. All the surfaces were rough and hard. Wood, metal, stone. Ouch.

The bench where she'd undressed looked about as good as it got. At least it had a thin padded seat. "There?"

He stood and walked toward her, that enormous cock bobbing up and down with each step. She tried to swallow the lump forming in her throat but it didn't budge.

Instead of sitting, like she expected him to do, he caught her shoulders in his big hands and eased her backward until the bench's seat pressed against the backs of her legs.

"Sit."

She sat.

He kneeled on the floor before her and rested his hands on her knees. His gaze lifted to her face. "I want to taste you."

Her pussy pulsed as blood drained from every other part of her and gathered there. Unable to speak, she nodded.

He eased her knees apart and leaned forward. His first touch was soft, teasing, tantalizing. It skirted around her labia, tickling her inner thighs. She sighed and let her legs part wider as her need grew more urgent.

Empty, tingly and wet, her pussy ached to be filled. And that bittersweet discomfort only increased when he parted her labia and flickered his warm, moist tongue over her clit.

Blades of heat pierced her body with each quick swipe of his tongue, and when he pressed two long fingers inside, she moaned in ecstasy.

She could hear her own juices as he hooked his fingers to scrape against the sensitive upper wall and plunged them in and out in a fierce finger-fuck. Instinctively, her body tensed as she felt the first tingles of an approaching climax. "Fuck me," she begged, her throat suddenly raw, her eyes closed tightly to shut out the world of sensations her mind couldn't register. She was lost in her need, her body, mind and spirit focused on only one thing, the need to be one with him. "Fuck me now."

He pulled his fingers out and curled them around her hand. "Touch yourself." He pulled her hand to her mound and laid it there. "Touch yourself for me."

Hungry for him and eager to be filled, she had no choice but to obey. She drew slow circles over her clit and listened as he unwrapped the rubber.

When she felt him pull her hips until her bottom hovered at the edge of the bench seat, and press his cock against her sensitive flesh, she drew her legs apart and her hand away.

"No. Leave it there," he growled.

It wasn't easy to do it but she did. With his thick rod pushing against her perineum, threatening to rip her, she had to concentrate on opening to him. She gasped as the head finally breached her tight tissues and slipped inside.

"God dammit, you're tight." He didn't move. She could hear his heavy breathing, hear his self-control slipping.

Sensations blurred, smells and sounds. The scents of chlorine and damp male skin and something else, something sharp and unpleasant, invaded her nose. But she didn't care at the moment.

The sounds of their mingled breathing and the distant sound of voices outside reached her ears but faded in and out of her awareness.

She inhaled deeply and something burned the back of her throat. She coughed, the action causing her to tighten her pussy walls around his thick cock.

He groaned and pushed deeper.

Suddenly, the sharp shrill of an alarm sounded in the room and she threw her arms around his shoulders and clung to him. Her eyelids lifted and her eyes instantly teared up, blurring her vision.

And then a shower of ice-cold water sprayed from the ceiling.

In unison, they yelled out, their bodies still joined, their heads tipped to the ceiling, "Oh no!"

Chapter Three

🔊

Despite being buried deep inside her, his erection turned flaccid, thanks to the cold shower and panicked voices shouting just outside the door. No doubt about it, some fireman would be barreling his way through any second now.

What a mood killer!

Speaking of killing, if Jeremy hadn't already been dead, she would have killed him by now.

The sprinklers shut off and the smoke cleared but it was too late. The damage had already been done.

Rafe looked disappointed and embarrassed as he pulled out. He remained silent as he dug through the contents of his bag, pulled out a pair of slightly damp underwear and shorts and dressed.

"I'm sorry about this," she said as she hurried to dress.

"It's not your fault."

She watched him teeter around the edge of the tub until he was on the wood deck rimming the back side. "It is, in a way."

He eyed the banana tree. "No, there's something I need to tell you. But first, do you think I'd kill this thing if I gave it a little shake?"

"I wonder if you give anything a *little* shake. Still, I doubt you could hurt that thing. I think it's fake." She drained the second glass of wine—no sense throwing it away, even if it was slightly diluted—and wrapped the glasses in her damp towel. All her things collected, she sat to put on her shoes.

He gave the tree a couple of good shakes and the shorts fell into his hands. "Hey! These are burned. How'd that happen? They were wet."

"Um. I have something I need to tell you too."

Not looking pleased, he balled up the ruined trunks and tossed them in the trash can next to the bench. "Whatever you have to say can't be as strange as what I have to tell you."

Confident it would, she challenged, "Care to put a wager on that?"

At least the smile returned. "Sure. What'll we bet?"

"How about…" She considered the possibilities and even though this date had ended in disaster, she couldn't help choosing something naughty for her prize. "How about the loser has to do anything—and I mean absolutely anything—the winner asks on our next date."

"You mean you want another one…um, date, that is?" He motioned toward the door. "Are you ready to leave?"

"Sure. And yes, I want another date if you do."

He unlocked the door and opened it for her. "You might change your mind when you hear this."

"You might change your mind too but I'm willing to take my chances." Sure she had him beat, she walked through the lobby, waved at the counter girl and a fireman on her way out and pushed open the main door to the parking lot. "Believe me, nothing could surprise me. So give, what's the big secret?"

He shook his head and opened her car door for her. "Not until you're sitting."

She tossed her bag on the back seat and sat then patted the passenger seat next to her. "Well, at least come sit in here with me. I promise, I won't slug you or anything, no matter what it is."

He pushed her door closed and rounded the car, finally lowering himself into the passenger seat. "Okay." He drew in a visible breath and exhaled but still said nothing.

"Oh, for God's sake it can't be that bad," she teased with a smile. "Oh my gosh! I got it, you're gay. Shoot! Why are all the good ones gay, like that cutie on Will and Grace? Please, just tell me you aren't gay and I'll be fine."

"Believe me, that's not the issue."

"Good." That minor question resolved, she prodded, "So, what is it?"

"You're going to laugh, but...I'm being haunted," he mumbled.

She couldn't have heard that right. "Huh?"

"I'm haunted."

"You? By whom?"

"Aren't you going to laugh and tell me I'm insane?"

"Why would I do that?"

"Because, outside of a few women who fancy themselves psychic mediums, every person I've told has either offered to escort me to the nearest hospital or laughed their ass off."

"I won't. I believe you, although I wouldn't mind losing a little on the posterior."

He looked pleased, relieved even. "Your posterior is perfect the way it is. So you believe me?"

"Yes. Where did your ghost come from? Is it a he ghost or a she ghost? Those things matter to some people."

"They do? I call her Annabelle and she somehow glommed onto me — or whatever ghosts do — when I went to a psychic to try to make peace with my dead father... This conversation is ridiculous."

"No, not ridiculous at all. I think it's interesting. How did you discover you were haunted?"

"I was on a date. For some reason, Annabelle's very jealous and gets a kick out of dumping water on any woman who comes within arm's reach of me. The poor woman went completely berserk. I had no idea what had happened. Then it happened again when I went on my next date — with someone else. And again...and I knew it couldn't be a coincidence." His grin grew quite wide and devilish when she didn't respond. "So, when do I get my prize?"

"Not so quick, buddy. You haven't heard my secret yet."

"It can't be more bizarre than a jealous she-devil who douses my dates."

"Oh, yes it can. You see, I'm also being haunted. By my ex-husband, Jeremy. But he doesn't use water, he uses fire to scare away my dates."

It took a moment for her words to sink in. She could tell by the lengthy blank stare and the eventual spark of realization that finally struck those deep mocha-colored eyes. His silence was followed by a round of deep belly laughs that shook her tiny car.

She enjoyed the sound of his laughter, the way it bounced around inside her tummy, the way it made his eyes sparkle like a child's. "Hey, I didn't laugh at you," she said, feigning insult. "Does that mean I win?"

"I'd say it was a draw but that makes us both winners...if we can figure out a way to keep ourselves out of the line of fire—literally."

"There has to be a way." Her gaze tangled with his and she caught a glimmer of determination on his face.

"Where would we be water-and fire-safe? Outside somewhere, maybe?"

"Oh no. I'm not an exhibitionist. What if someone sees us?"

"That just adds to the excitement."

"Isn't dodging flames and cascading water enough excitement for you? Not to mention, of course, the obvious." She felt her cheeks blushing.

He reached forward and pinched one. "Pink's definitely your color."

She gave his hand a playful swat and it fell from her face and landed in her lap.

He didn't move it. "If we're going to outwit these devious little spirits, we're going to have to be a little daring."

"I've never even gotten a parking ticket."

His fingers slowly curled and uncurled, tickling her mound. "How long has it been since you've had sex?"

"Too long." It was getting mighty hot in the car. She shifted, settling lower in the seat and opened her legs just a bit.

"Did you like the way I felt inside you?" His hand slid lower and rubbed harder.

She opened the window and fanned her face with her hand. "Couldn't you tell?" She sucked in a quick breath when she thought she'd caught the scent of burning cloth. "Uh...better check your shorts."

"They are a little snug, thanks to my—"

"No, I think they're burning again!"

He looked at her blankly, obviously having forgotten what she'd told him about Jeremy, so she grabbed him by the shoulders, yanked him against her and planted her lips to his. She didn't bother with the small stuff but went straight for the gusto. She pushed her tongue into his mouth and savored his flavor. Her hands reached around and traveled up his neck and she tangled her fingers in his thick waves. She felt herself heating up from the inside out.

Then the expected happened. A gush of freezing water saturated them.

His lips still pressed firmly to hers, he sucked in a gasp of surprise as he took the full brunt of the downpour. His head and massive upper body covered much of her face and chest but from belly down, she got a soaking. The water's almost freezing temperature cooled all the parts that had been heated by that searing kiss.

"Damn it, Annabelle," he grumbled. Looking cute, disappointed, even a little annoyed, he ran his long fingers through his sodden hair. It spiked up, going this way and that.

"You ought to thank her. If she hadn't doused us just now, you'd be suffering from third-degree burns. I'm afraid I owe you another pair of shorts."

"Oh." He chuckled. "Next time, I'll just have to make sure I'm not wearing any. He can't burn what I'm not wearing."

That statement sent a pleasant mental picture into her head.

"I'd say that look suggests you wouldn't mind."

"Heck, no. What woman would?"

"Then are you with me?"

"In regards to?"

"Tomorrow? I think I have the perfect place but I need to check the weather forecast."

"Why? If it's raining, what's the difference?"

He smiled. "True. In fact, I'm hoping it's supposed to rain. At least that way, the location I have in mind'll be a little less crowded."

"Little less crowded? What kind of place are you suggesting that's crowded on a Sunday afternoon?"

"You, my dear," he poked her nose and opened the car door, "will just have to wait to find out. Pleasant dreams." He leaned closer, suggesting he wanted to give her another kiss, but she tipped her head back, not wanting to risk another fire or flood. She wasn't sure her car would start as it was.

Instead she blew him a kiss. "We better wait until tomorrow. What time?"

"How about I pick you up at one?"

"That's fine. What'll I wear?"

"How about something waterproof?"

She shivered. Between the loss of his body heat and the cooling effects of her soaking wet clothes, she was freezing. Her teeth chattered as she stuttered, "Good idea."

Her car started without a problem.

* * * * *

That night, she was forced to sleep with her head under the pillow, which she'd heard wasn't good for one's brain—something about lack of oxygen. Jeremy was at it again.

The man wasn't only costing her sex but grey matter as well. This time he was making loud thumping noises over her head all night long.

Didn't ghosts need to sleep too?

The next morning, she dragged her exhausted body out of bed, waiting as late as she dared, and showered. Assuming she'd be drenched again, she used the waterproof makeup again and didn't spend a whole lot of time on her hair. However, she did select her clothing carefully. A loose and flowing knee-length skirt with no panties underneath—she felt scandalous!—a snug knit pullover top, some sandals and a rain poncho and she was all set.

Her pussy was already moist and ready as well. There was something very sexy and fun about the feeling of a silky skirt brushing against her bare bottom.

It was a gorgeous day, so she waited for him outside on the little bench next to the front door. Considering the weather, she knew she had to look silly wearing the bright yellow poncho. There wasn't a cloud in the sky and no rain in the forecast for the next few days.

So she looked like an idiot. Wouldn't be the first time. Wouldn't be the last time either.

He came outside a few minutes later. Clad in a pair of cotton sweat pants, a T-shirt that clung to his sculpted chest like a harlot, and a pair of running shoes, he looked ready to head to the gym, not on a date.

"I'm overdressed." She stood and reached for her door.

"Oh, no. It's perfect," he purred, the sultry undercurrent in his voice halting her instantly. "Are you wearing panties?"

"No."

He licked his lips. "Good. Let's go end our abstinence. Between the two of us, it's probably been a year since we've had sex." He opened his car door for her.

She sat. Her stiff plastic parka puffed out in front of her like an oversized baby bib. She patted it down against her body. "At least."

He shut the door, rounded the front of the car and sat next to her in the driver's seat. "Ready?"

"For anything you have to offer, stud." She gave him a wink. "As long as it doesn't involve breaking any laws, that is. Where are we going?" She fastened her seatbelt.

"To a place where a little excess water and fire won't cause a problem."

"Such a place exists?"

"You bet it does." He started the car and backed out of the driveway then put the car into gear and drove down the street. "Did you bring those rubbers?"

"Sure did."

"Good, though there won't be any banana trees for me to lose my shorts in where we're going."

"Sounds intriguing. No banana trees, and fire- and water-proof. A cave?"

"Nope."

"I'm stumped. Want to give me a hint or two?"

"No. What fun would that be? Let's talk about more important things, like our lives, our dreams, our wishes."

"Not a single hint?"

"Nope. Now on with it. Tell me about your life."

"Okay, if you insist. Let's see." She glanced out the window and watched a line of houses go by as the car carried her toward the freeway. "My life is dull—outside of the ex-thing. My dreams are bizarre—"

"Where do you work?" he interrupted. "We've lived next to each other for so long but you've never told me. And I promise we'll get back to those bizarre dreams later. I like the sound of those."

"I'm a secretary in a sales office. I work for a bunch of lazy guys who play golf with automotive engineers and call it work. What about you?"

"I play golf with lazy sales guys. But I don't call it work. I work a lot of overtime and take comp days."

"You're an engineer?"

He nodded. "Yep. At Ford."

"Good thing I didn't say anything else."

"You weren't about to bad-mouth my employer, were you?" he asked in a teasing voice.

"Oh, no way. Love Ford. Love all our customers."

He eyed her with skepticism.

"Really. I'm being honest. I enjoy my job, though I wouldn't mind being a lazy sales guy—er, woman—who plays golf someday."

"What's stopping you?"

"Don't have an engineering degree and I suck at golf but I love the game."

"Even though all your competitors' sales reps probably have engineering degrees that doesn't mean you couldn't do their job. And most people stink at golf unless they play regularly. I could give you some pointers if you like. My game isn't too bad."

"That would be fun! Er, but I don't have any equipment, clubs or those nifty saddle shoes with the cleats on the bottom. Heck, I don't even have any balls."

"Not a problem. You can use my balls." He chuckled. "That sounded...wrong. Let me try that again. We can take care of the equipment issue without too much trouble. How about playing a round next weekend? It's impossible to get a tee-time on the public courses around here on the weekends but I'm a member of a private course not too far away. Hope you don't mind playing later in the day, though. The die hards play early in the morning so they can be with their families in the afternoon. Later in the day you can usually get in without too much of a problem."

"Sounds great to me."

"Good. It's a date then." He looked as pleased as she felt.

Things were going great. Not only was she feeling the chemistry—which couldn't be missed by a deaf, blind, mute person—but she also sensed a deeper connection forming, a comfort she hadn't shared with anyone in a long time, if ever. She felt...at home.

And the best part—Jeremy hadn't made a peep all morning.

Yes-siree, this was a good day. No Jeremy banging, stomping, thudding or lighting fires. Water wasn't falling from the sky. And she was on her way to some unknown destination to have sex with the handsomest, sexiest man on earth.

Only one thing would make it better. If those first two changes could be forever. If only she could freely reach out and touch that tan-skinned arm mere inches from her without fearing a catastrophe. It would be so nice to twine her fingers with his or lift his arm up and wrap it around her shoulder so she could snuggle in close.

There had to be a way.

Where were the Ghostbusters when a desperate, sex-starved woman needed them?

They drove up the freeway exit ramp and she rolled down the window some more, catching the unmistakable scent of the lake in the air. She stuck her nose into the wind and inhaled. "Smells wonderful."

"We're almost there."

He turned down a wooded driveway and stopped at a little wooden toll booth. There was a sign on the front. Michigan Metro Park.

"Oh no, you've got to be kidding. We're going to have sex at a park? Don't trees and grass burn?"

He shot her one of his trademark wicked grins, the one she was beginning to adore and crave more than chocolate—she craved chocolate constantly. "We aren't going into the woods."

"We can't do it on the beach with thousands of people around us. Besides, we'll stick out like sore thumbs. I didn't wear my bathing suit."

"No, this skirt is better than a bathing suit." He reached toward her but pulled his hand back before touching her thigh. "I can't wait to get you out of this car," he growled.

He parked the car in the crowded lot and got out. After opening her door, he went to the trunk and gathered several blankets, a cooler—when had he put that in there?—and a gym bag.

"This is insane."

"No, insanity is letting a couple of dead people keep us from being happy."

"Happy? We're just talking about sex here...aren't we? I mean, don't get me wrong, I love sex as much as the next girl." She fell into step beside him. "But is it worth going to jail for? Is that happiness?"

"We won't go to jail. Trust me."

Her hand itched to reach out and take his but she resisted. Their arms occasionally brushed as they walked over a grassy hill toward the beach. There were hundreds of bodies dotting the beach, shoreline and lake. Children, families. This was no place for a midafternoon fuckfest.

"This is wrong."

"Trust me."

"You keep telling me that."

"And I'll keep repeating it until you do." When they reached the water's edge, he pointed toward a copse of trees. "This way."

"I think we determined that the woods was a bad idea."

"We aren't going into the woods." He motioned her to follow him down a narrow path that was little more than a narrow band of beaten-down weeds.

At least he was headed away from the kids with arm floaties and their mommies and daddies. The thought of some curious preschooler's parent screaming, "You've disturbed my child for life!" when she toddled over and witnessed their less-than-wholesome behavior had her quite bothered. She'd rather risk fire or flood, to be honest.

The woods gave way to a secluded clearing rimmed on one side by tall, craggy rocks and the other three by more trees. It was secluded, peaceful, quiet.

He motioned toward the rocks. "This way."

"On the rocks? Couldn't we find a…softer place?" She cringed as she imagined her spine being ground into the jagged surface of the nearest boulder. It didn't look the least bit comfy.

He smiled over his shoulder. "Trust me."

It was hard to trust anyone who had such a devious sparkle in his eye all the time. "Hey, buddy. In my world only a sucker hands over trust after only one date."

"This may only be our second date but we've practically lived together for over a year now. We can hardly call each other strangers."

"No, I guess you're right."

They climbed up, over and through the rocks. He occasionally helped her steady herself as she stumbled and tripped her way along behind him. Sandals were not the ideal footwear for rock climbing.

This had better be worth it.

They finally reached a cozy little cove at the water's edge. Surrounded on three sides by towering rocks, it was just a tiny patch of sand, a private oasis of sorts. On the fourth side stretched the sparkling water.

He handed her a blanket and she spread it on the sand then sat to remove her sandals.

Enjoying the way the sun flashed gold on the water, she leaned back on her elbows and allowed herself a moment to enjoy it. "This is wonderful. How'd you find this place?"

"Saw it once when I was on a friend's boat out on the lake." He dragged one foot in the sand as he walked a wide circle around the blanket then set four metal pails in the sand at equal intervals and lit four fires. The sharp scent of burning paper drifted to her nose. He pulled a damp bottle of wine and two glasses out of the cooler then sat next to her. "Thirsty? I brought a something very special for today."

"Oh yeah? What's the occasion?" she teased, watching him work at the cork with a corkscrew. Yow, mama did that man have some arms. The twisting motion showed off his muscles to perfection just like before. She wondered if a daily bottle of wine might be beyond moderation. She could watch him do that every day.

He pulled the cork free of the bottle, poured two glasses then set the bottle back in the cooler. "I'll tell you later. How about a toast?" He pulled out a handful of red flower petals and scattered them over the blanket then lifted his glass in a toast.

"Sure."

"To overcoming devious spirits and battling elements."

"Amen." She touched her glass to his then took a drink. The wine was unbelievably smooth. Sweet. Delicious. "This is heavenly. What is it?"

"Massandra 1955 White Port Surozh."

"Wow. So old. I've never drunk a wine older than I am."

He took a swallow, set his glass down and leaned closer. The way he was leaning on his outstretched arms, and the tilt of his head and angle of his eyes, he reminded her of a wildcat. "Do you know anything about the Massandra collection?"

She felt her heart pitter-pattering. "Not a thing."

"The winery is old, built in the 1800s. It's built into the side of mountains near Yalta, with long tunnels bored deep into the mountainside." On all fours, he prowled closer. When he reached her side, she half expected him to pounce on her.

"Is that so?" She took another drink then set her glass down too.

"Yes. It's said those tunnels keep the wine at the optimum temperature."

"I'm about at my optimum temperature myself," she heard herself say. She lifted the rain poncho over her head, folded it into a neat pile and set it on the sand.

"Good." He crawled over top her, forcing her to lie back on the blanket. His chest pressed against hers and his knee wedged between her bent legs. Her skirt fluttered in the breeze and settled high on her hip.

One of his hands followed its path, resting on her hipbone while the other one palmed her cheek. His thumb tickled her bottom lip and she instinctively opened her mouth and drew it inside.

It tasted salty and sweet, a combination she'd never been able to resist. In fact, in many ways he epitomized her most favorite combinations, her deepest weaknesses. He was strong yet gentle. Firm yet yielding. Intelligent yet reachable. Gorgeous yet humble.

He was the kind of man she'd dreamed of meeting since she'd played her first game of prince and princess with Larry Larson on the kindergarten playground.

His kiss was slow and undemanding but thorough, and while his mouth worked magic, his hands pushed her shirt up, unhooked the front clasp of her bra and explored her breasts and stomach.

She heard her breathing quicken before she felt it, almost as if she'd been outside her own body. Growing groggy-headed and dizzy, she forced herself to take a long, steady breath. The scents of man and lake and nature filled her nostrils, all wonderful, sweet scents that she savored.

She enjoyed the way he tasted too, a heady combination of wine and him.

His hand delved between her thighs, parted her labia and stroked her pussy as his kiss grew more demanding. His tongue thrust in and out of her mouth. She felt the muscles of his arms harden under her fingertips as she gripped them.

The need within her spiraled round and round, growing slowly and then building quicker as he stroked and kissed and whispered sweet words in her ear.

He stopped for a split second then returned, spreading a smooth, garlicky salve down her stomach.

"Garlic?" she asked, too drunk with passion to really care.

"Trust me." He pushed two fingers inside her pussy and she cried out in ecstasy. His kiss muffled her voice, closed it off, as she called out again. Her pussy walls closed tightly around his fingers, intensifying the pleasure his finger-fuck gave her with each thrust.

He broke the kiss and instead used his mouth in a more intimate place. His tongue alternately flickered lightly over her clit and swirled slowly in soft circles as his fingers curled inside her pussy. A third finger pressed at her anus.

It was all too much yet it wasn't enough. She needed to breathe. She needed release.

"Fuck me now."

"No. Net yet."

"Yes, now." She tangled her fingers in his hair and pulled. "I won that bet. You have to do what I say."

"I won too." He dropped his head again and continued laving her pussy with his tongue. Two fingers slid into her pussy and a third fucked her ass.

The man was bound and determined to drive her insane!

She thrashed, fighting the burning climax threatening to carry her away. "I won and I say fuck me now."

"Well, I can't say I've ever had a woman ask me like that before."

She felt him shifting above her then heard the crinkle of plastic as he unwrapped the rubber.

Finally he pulled down the front of his pants just enough to expose his thick cock and rolled on the rubber. As he leaned forward, it pressed against her pussy, begging admittance.

She held her breath against the burn as it slowly sank inside. When they were completely joined, she clung to his shoulders and met his thrust with one of her own, their hips working in unison.

She tipped her head forward and tasted his neck. Salty again.

He groaned.

She lifted her legs up and wrapped them tightly around his hips to take him deeper, and moaned as his cock grated against the sensitive upper walls as it pistoned in and out.

His breathing rasped against her cheek as he eased the pace of their lovemaking. "Need to slow down."

"What for?"

He smiled and brushed her hair away from her face. "For you."

"I'm doing fine." She giggled. "I certainly have no complaints."

"Good." His cock still deep inside, he sat upright and pulled her legs wide apart. "Now, remember that fantasy you told me about?"

"Yes."

"Show me how you would pleasure yourself for me."

"Don't take it out."

"I won't. I'm going to fuck you and we're going to come together."

"Okay."

"Now, do what I say and touch your pussy."

She slid a hand down the flat of her stomach and rested the base of her palm on her mound. Her fingertip traced slow circles around her clit.

"That's it, baby. Show me your pussy. Spread your legs wider."

She did as he asked, spreading them until the muscles of her inner thighs burned as they stretched.

His cock began to slowly pump in and out again, and that combined with her own touches built a powerful tension that stole her breath away and drove her mad. Her only focus was on finding the pinnacle that was just beyond reach. She could feel it nearing with every thrust, with every touch, with every thump of her racing heart.

Her body tightened, even her feet cramped.

"That's it, baby. I want to see you come. I want to hear your cries of release. Bathe my cock in your sweet juices."

She felt the heat well up from deep inside and spread out and with a cry, she tumbled into the stars. Colors flashed in the dark as she hurtled through the galaxy, carried on a current of sweet bliss. She heard him cry out in his release and felt him stiffen before pressing down on her chest and stomach. His weight grew heavier. His breaths puffed ragged and quick against her neck and shoulder.

He kissed her neck and collarbone and cradled her in his arms.

And only after the heat of their lovemaking cooled to a mild simmer did she realize one thing—there hadn't been any flames, outside of the ones they had stirred in each other. And there hadn't been any water, outside of the tears she felt slipping from the corner of her eye and the gentle waves lapping at her feet.

Somehow, they'd defeated the ghosts. But how?

Chapter Four

ဆ

"Am I dreaming or are they gone?" Stephanie whispered, afraid if she said it too loud she might catch a formerly distracted ghost's attention.

Rafe rolled her onto her back and settled his hips between her legs. The tip of his erect cock pressed against her vulva. "Shall we try for round two and double-check?"

She giggled. "Do we dare? We might be testing our luck. Maybe they were napping...Uh, do ghosts sleep? I didn't think that Jeremy did, at least not at night when I wanted to," she rambled.

"I think it was the wine," he said as he trailed little kisses and nibbles down her neck and along her collarbone.

Goose bumps bloomed over her upper body and she shivered. "Wine? You got ghosts drunk? How'd you manage that?"

"Not exactly." He shifted his weight back until he was kneeling between her legs and her upper torso was completely uncovered. The sun was warm on her skin, a delightful contrast to the chill from his tickling touches to her neck and shoulders.

Feeling like a cat lazing in a sunny window, she lifted her arms overhead and stretched. Her breasts rose into the air as she drew in a deep breath and she was not surprised to see Rafe take full advantage of her position.

He lowered himself over top of her, capturing her hands in one of his, and lapped at her nipple. "I think the Russian spirit might've scared them away."

She sighed with contentment, arched her back to press her boobs higher into the air and ruminated the power of Russian spirits, in more ways than one. The glass of wine she'd drunk a while back was still making her feel a little flushed. "What spirit? The alcohol?"

He turned his attention to the other breast, drawing slow circles around the nipple with his tongue. "Mikhail Semenovich Vorontsov."

"That's a mouthful."

He suckled her breast and she bit back a groan of pleasure. "Not as much a mouthful as these." He kneaded her breasts then pinched her nipples until she was breathless with need.

"That was sad," she teased, referring to his quip, even as she wallowed in the pleasure he so generously offered her. Waves of longing pulsed out from her center, warming each part as it rippled outward. What magic that man could perform with his tongue and teeth, not to mention his other parts.

"Sad? How'd you know how Vorontsov died?" he asked, now gently nibbling one nipple while tugging on the other one with thumb and forefinger.

In all her years, her breasts had never seen such thorough loving. Although it was extremely enjoyable, it was also very frustrating. There were parts further south that were feeling neglected. "I didn't..." she said, having difficulty following the conversation. She'd never been the kind who could chitchat while she fucked. For some reason, her grey matter shut down once certain nerve endings were stimulated. Neck, pussy and boobs. Those were the ones sure to put her into a catatonic state.

"Then what's sad?"

"Oh…nothing. Whoever he was, I'll have to thank him later." Eager for Rafe's touch between her legs, she tangled her fingers in his hair and wrapped her legs around his waist. "Don't you think it's time to maybe get on with things?"

He stopped torturing her breasts for a minute and smiled, leaning low until his nose nearly touched hers. "Not yet. I'm enjoying myself. I like watching you squirm in agony." He winked.

She smacked his chest. Not hard, just enough to make a nice, crisp slapping sound. "You're a cruel bastard."

He caught her hand and leaning forward, pinned it to the ground above her head, along with the other one. "You don't know the meaning of the word cruel but you're about to find out."

"Now that sounds promising. When do we begin?" She wriggled under him, making a concentrated effort at stimulating his balls, which, thanks to his position over top of her, were just above her stomach. With an arch of her spine, she was able to make contact with them. And some coordinated stomach muscle maneuvers created a fair amount of friction.

He gave her a dissatisfied grunt, which satisfied her immensely. But then he shifted his position so she'd need a spine of rubber to reach any part of him that mattered. "We'll get to the cruelty thing soon. And you're going to pay dearly, love. First, I want to talk about Vorontsov."

"Now? Why's some dead Russian guy so important that we must talk about him right this minute? I'm much more interested in the paying dearly part." Her arms still pinned firmly overhead, she gave him an encouraging nod and lifted her legs to try and wrap them around his waist again.

"Because he—combined with a few odds and ends I got from the psychic—cured our curse."

"And I'm sure you can see how very grateful I am. Can't we get on with the celebration?"

"I got him in this bottle of wine. Cost me a fortune. I think that psychic is a shady character. She charges to get you haunted and then charges more to cure you." Pulling her hands together, he secured them with one hand and reached for the bottle of wine with the other. He lifted the bottle into the air in a silent toast to somebody—maybe the dead guy—took several swallows then poured a tiny puddle onto the middle of her stomach. He licked it off with a tongue that moved in ways she never would've guessed a human's tongue could, then lowered his mouth to kiss her. He tasted sweet and spicy, like the wine. His tongue dipped into her mouth and she savored his flavor until her breathing grew ragged and uneven. Then he broke the kiss. "Isn't that interesting? She sold me a dead Russian general in an old wine bottle. She said he'd protect us."

Frustrated beyond belief, she muttered, "A ghost in a wine bottle? It's...unexpected. What else did she sell you? A fairy in a pickle jar? Or maybe...oh..." The words she'd been about to say melted away as she watched him set the wine bottle down, reach between her legs and find her slit. Unfortunately, his light touches to her vulva did nothing but intensify the burning need churning deep inside her. She moaned.

"What, love? A devil in a soda can?" he asked on a chuckle.

"I can see that nasty little devil's been released."

He scooted down lower, his head hovering above her pussy. "And about to do his naughtiest deed."

"I like naughty." Aware of what was about to happen, she let her eyelids fall closed and her legs open to accommodate him.

"So do I." He parted her pussy's outer lips with his fingers then flicked his tongue over her clit. The light, teasing touches sent bolts of pleasure zipping through her body, up toward her head, down to her toes, zigzagging everywhere in between. It felt like there were hundreds of little electrical currents buzzing through her body. As he continued, the little bolts became more intense, until she was dragging in uneven, heavy breaths, and soft moans slipped over her tongue with every exhalation. "That's it, baby." He slid first one then two fingers inside and hooked them until his knuckles gently scraped the sensitive upper wall.

It was all she could do to refrain from screaming out. But in the back of her mind, she remembered they were outside, where shouts would travel far and possibly bring a host of unwanted spectators, living and dead alike. Instead, she bit down on her lip and gripped the blanket underneath her in two tense fists.

He stopped teasing her clit with his tongue and she swore she'd die if he didn't start again. "I'm going to go slow this time. I want to enjoy every moment."

"No, no, no! Please don't stop."

"Patience, love. We have all our lives to enjoy each other. Let's take our time." He pistoned his fingers in and out several times then pulled them completely out. "Will you do something for me now?"

In a haze of need, she waited but he didn't speak. He didn't touch her either. Finally, she opened her eyes. "What do you want me to do?"

"Will you take me in your mouth?"

Her pussy throbbed as she imagined his cock slipping past her lips, his fingers twined in her hair, his hands gently urging her to take him deeper into her throat. "Yes, oh yes."

As if in a show of appreciation, he kissed her first. His tongue slipped into her mouth and twisted around her tongue, sharing the flavors of wine and her intimate parts. It was the most erotic, sensual flavor. She couldn't get enough. As they kissed, he gently helped her sit up. Then he broke the kiss and kneeled before her, his glorious cock there for her pleasure.

She was shy at first, gently cradling his balls in one hand while closing her fist around his cock. She yearned for him to take control, to push his thick cock into her mouth, to take her head in his hands and dictate her every movement. Curious to see how he was reacting, she tipped her head and glanced up.

His face was a mask of tension. The lines of his jaw and neck were severe, drawn so tight they looked comical. He didn't speak a word.

"Show me," she said softly. "I want to please you."

His eyelids heavy, he groaned and stroked her hair. As he nodded, he put one hand under his cock and lifted the tip to her lips. With the other hand, he pressed on the back of her head until her mouth was full of sweet cock.

Eager to taste every bit of him, she twirled her tongue round and round the ridge at the head. She sucked and slurped, using her hand positioned against her lips, as an extension of her mouth. Slowly she relaxed her throat to take him deeper, deeper. Her pussy throbbed as his groans of pleasure reached her ears.

A tug at the back of her head made her pull away but no sooner did the tip of his cock slip through her lips than it was pushed back inside, deep into her throat.

"Yes, baby. That's it. I love how you love me. You take all of me," he chanted as he thrust his cock inside her mouth. One hand reached down to her breast. His fingers found her nipple and pinched, just hard enough to make her squirm with hunger. Her pussy was so achingly wet, she had to fill it. Seeing no other option, she reached one hand between her legs and touched herself. "Oh yes," Rafe encouraged her. "Touch yourself as you take me in your mouth. Damn, you're so sexy. Now kneel. I want to fuck your mouth and slap your ass."

He didn't have to make that suggestion twice. She felt like she'd been freed, and not just free of the ghost who'd been haunting her for eons, but free from her reservations, free from old ideas about what sex was supposed to be. She was free to explore, to enjoy, to have fun!

This was the way she wanted to spend the rest of her life, on her hands and knees, Rafe's cock, hands and mouth giving her pleasure like she'd never known. Touching, stroking, kissing, biting.

He gently thrust his cock into her mouth, at the same time reaching over her back, lifting her skirt and striking her ass with an open hand. A sharp slap sound cut through the air, making her jump slightly. Then the sting followed, not painful, just enough to quicken her heart rate. Her empty pussy pulsed.

The second strike was just as sharp but he followed it with a gentle stroke. What a reward! Her mouth full of cock, she moaned with gratitude.

The third smack to her rear end was softer and the caress to her ass lasted much longer, until she was literally melting and felt her elbows and knees would give out.

He pulled his cock from her mouth and kissed her, his tongue taking its place, thrusting in and out in a constant rhythm. Unsteady, her entire being—body, soul and spirit—begging for completion, she reached up and clung to his shoulders. Eager to feel skin against skin, she leaned forward and pressed her chest against his.

"I want to fuck you from behind." He pressed on her shoulders, coaxing her to kneel back down. Shuddering, she complied. Her pussy was throbbing relentlessly, so wet that moisture was trailing down the inside of her thighs. "I want to touch your ass while I fuck you. Can I?" On his knees as well, he urged her to turn around.

"Yes, oh yes." Facing away from him, her tingling ass pressed against his groin, her fingers sinking into warm sand, she let her head fall forward. Breathless, she waited for him to sink his cock deep into her pussy. Her entire body, every minute part, awaited that magic moment.

"Shoot! I need another rubber."

She didn't look up as she felt him move away from her. Instead, she concentrated on every sensation as it penetrated the haze of need that cocooned her. The scents of water, sand, sex and man...and garlic...the glitter of red and gold lights behind her closed eyelids. The feel of the woolen blanket under her knees and the smooth sand under her palms, sifting through her fingers. The heat of the sun striking her back as he pushed her shirt up toward her shoulders. Even the crinkling of the rubber packaging was erotic at the moment.

She was thrilled to feel the heat of his skin as it pressed against the backs of her thighs.

"I've waited so long for this moment. I didn't even know how much I've wanted it until now," Rafe said, lifting her skirt again.

"I did." She dug her fingers into the sand. "Fuck me. Please. Now." She held her breath.

He pressed his cock against her perineum but didn't penetrate her. "Just tell me one thing. I need to hear you say it. Tell me this won't be the last time. Tell me we're going to be together, in all ways."

"Yes, oh yes. I want that too."

"Good." He buried his cock deep inside her pussy and she gasped, thankful for the instant feeling of fullness but equally eager to feel his withdrawal so she could enjoy the next thrust.

To maximize the sensation, she tightened her inside muscles around him. The result was a low groan from both of them.

He pulled out slowly, inch by delectable inch, then thrust back inside. Thanks to the angle of his hips, the head of his cock pushed against the back wall of her vagina as it sunk deep inside, creating a current of warmth that pulsed up and out from her center. Her arms began trembling.

"You're so tight, love. So hot and wet and tight." He drove his cock deep inside her, over and over and she rocked back to meet his every thrust.

She bit back a cry as he pulled her ass cheeks apart with his fingers, then teased her anus. This was both heaven and hell, pleasure and pain. She wanted fulfillment yet strained to hold back, wishing to enjoy every heartbeat, every stroke, every sigh.

Seeming to sense how close she was, he slowed his pace. What were wild thrusts became languid intimate caresses. Then he pulled out, scooted away and sat on the blanket. He had a naughty, sexy grin as he motioned for her to come to him. "I want to watch you come," he said in a low growl.

Raising her skirt, she lowered herself onto his cock until her rear end was resting on his thighs and his rigid shaft was as deep as it could go. They moaned in unison as she rhythmically tightened and relaxed her pussy, the muscles milking him. Their gazes locked, they moved as one, kissing, touching, caressing, bringing each other to the throes of climax then slowing just enough to avoid coming. Yet, even though they were physically joined, she craved more closeness, wished she could literally climb into his skin with him. The best she could do was loop her arms around his neck and lean forward until her breasts were pressed flat against his chest. She gripped the hair at the back of his head and dropped her head back.

He whispered, "No, look at me. Don't close me out."

It wasn't easy but she lifted her head and opened her eyes. She felt almost drugged, as if all the sounds, smells, tastes and sights of lovemaking were a potent spell, not only burning her from the inside out but pulling her from her body.

His eyelids were heavy too, partially covering his dark brown irises, as he gazed back at her. And his expression was strained as though he was clinging to his self-control by a thread. It might snap at any moment, just as hers was about to. As if it might help, she bit her lower lip.

He reached up and traced her lip with his fingertip and she opened her mouth to draw it into her mouth. His gaze turned fiery as he guided her hips up and down with his free hand and watched her suckle his finger.

That was it. She'd had enough waiting, had enough torture. She wanted release. Now. Working against the pace he was guiding her at, she sped up. Her arms braced against his shoulders as leverage, she rocked back and forth on him. His cock was deep, her pussy grating against his groin, creating a delightful friction against her clit. Her breaths filled her lungs in short gasps and emptied them in even shorter puffs. Her chest and stomach flushed. Her blood pounded in her ears. She stared at his face, his kiss-dampened mouth and hunger-filled eyes, and came.

Small tremors turned into huge quakes as the long-awaited orgasm pulsed through her body. The shaking and glorious waves seemed to last an eternity as she clung to him, gasping.

Just as they started to slow, she felt the muscles under the skin of his shoulders tighten. He grasped her hips, lifted them slightly then drove his cock up into her pussy in a frenzy of quick thrusts, each one met with a loud huff, as he found his own release. The motion intensified the spasms of her orgasm until she couldn't help crying out. She rode wave upon wave of fluid, pulsing heat until she was exhausted and satisfied.

Her body racked with tingles and twitches, she clung to him and drew in slow, deep breaths. The scents of man and sex filled her nostrils. Giddy, she smiled and kissed his chest. "That was... Wow."

"Yeah. Wow is right. I never thought... I mean I hoped..." One arm wrapped protectively around her neck, he stroked her back. "I've watched you, waiting for the chance to touch you. I've dreamed of feeling your hair slide through my fingertips, hearing you speak my name. I've wanted to gather you into my arms and hold you, to listen to your heartbeat and your soft breathing in the dark when I wake up and can't fall back asleep. I've wanted to see that look in your eyes again, the one you gave me the day you fell in the swimming pool."

"You have not." Her cheeks warming, one side of her face resting against his chest, she swatted at him. "You're just saying that to make me feel better."

"Better about what? Making love?" He cupped her chin and gently lifted it until she looked up at his face.

She had to admit, he looked genuinely confused. "Better about making love and then ditching me," she explained.

His expression changed from bemused to exasperated. "Ditching you? There's no way in hell I'm letting you go that easy. So don't even try pulling some escape act. It won't work. For one, I know where you live."

She almost couldn't believe what she was hearing. It was as if he'd read her mind and knew what words to speak to melt her heart. As she bent her head again, closed her eyes and listened to the steady thump, thump of his heart, she felt herself falling in love, falling harder than she'd ever allowed herself to before. "I was afraid to believe any of this could ever happen."

"You have nothing to be afraid of now. I'm sure the ghosts are gone."

At the moment, his cock deep still inside, his bulk pressed firmly against her, his right arm wrapped around her waist, she felt adored and protected, free to speak what she'd hidden even from herself. "Jeremy wasn't the only reason why I was afraid. In fact, he was sort of my guardian, now that I think about it. Since the end of that marriage I've been fearful."

"Of what?" he asked, continuing to shower her head and neck with little tickly kisses. "What were you most afraid of?" His cock was still deep inside her but he remained still. The intimate contact left her feeling very close to him, very vulnerable yet connected too, not just physically but emotionally and spiritually as well.

"I guess I didn't want to be hurt again. I didn't want to suffer another broken heart, feel that horrible, sick nauseous churning in my belly the moment when I saw that look in a man's eye again — the look that said he didn't care about me anymore. Maybe I let Jeremy stick around — heck, for all I know I forced him to stick around — as a safeguard against heartbreak. If I couldn't sleep with a man, he wouldn't get close. And if I didn't get close, I couldn't be hurt."

"I understand. In a way, Annabelle did the same for me," he admitted. "I can't talk to you this way. I need to see your eyes." He pulled his semi-flaccid cock from her body, disposed of the condom in a paper bag, pulled up his pants and backed away from her, palming her face between his hands. His thumbs gently stroked her lips. "She was a convenient scapegoat, a way for me to avoid what I wasn't ready to face yet. But I'm not afraid anymore."

"Neither am I."

"I want this—us—to work. That's why I went back to that psychic. I didn't know if her spell would work. Who would've thought some garlic, a circle drawn in the sand, an old bottle of wine and little bit of fire would chase away a ghost? I hoped it would. I didn't want to take a chance of losing you. I have a feeling this is going to be more than either of us expected."

"Me too."

"I want to fall asleep every night by your side and wake up with you beside me every morning. I want to make love to you and spoil you and romance you until your every fear is a distant memory and you can't remember a day spent without me. I want to visit this place ten, fifteen, twenty years from now and relive this day."

That was it. What woman stood a chance against a man who had so much heart, so much passion? He had her heart, whether he knew it or not.

"Just promise me one thing," she whispered as she leaned in and clung to him. "If something happens one day and, God forbid, you die before I do, promise me you'll haunt me to my last day."

"It's a promise." He gathered her into his arms and held her close.

They spent the rest of the afternoon celebrating by making love. They talked in their secret oasis in the park, about life and love and the future. And they joked about converting their duplex back into a single family residence.

They would paint one bedroom red for Jeremy and one bedroom blue for Annabelle, just in case they decided to return for a visit, which they both agreed was unlikely.

If nothing else, the rooms would be a tribute to two spirits who'd done what was necessary to bring them together, by trying to keep them apart.

Fire and water couldn't keep them apart and they had proven it.

The End

Phantasmic Fantasies

৪৩

Trademarks Acknowledgement

~

The author acknowledges the trademarked status and trademark owners of the following wordmarks mentioned in this work of fiction:

eBay: eBay Inc.

Barbie: Mattel, Inc.

Taser: Taser Systems, Inc

Krogers: Kroger Co. of Michigan, The

Discovery Channel: Discovery Communications, Inc.

UPS: United Parcel Service of America, Inc.

Mercedes: Daimler-Benz Aktiengesellschaft

Food Network: Television Food Network, G.P.

Ben & Jerry's: Ben & Jerry's Homemade, Inc.

Prologue

ട

There's no two ways about it. Dead guys have it rough.

First, there's the TV remote control issue. A dead guy has absolutely no chance of getting control of that little electronic wonder, and thus we're forced to watch those boring medical programs on the Discovery Channel during Monday night football games or movies on Lifetime Television during spring training pre-Season baseball games.

Can you say "Yawn"?

Second, if our hostess knows of our existence, which my last one did, she'll blame every little mishap or wiring short circuit on you. This was a real problem for me until recently. You see, my hostess just happened to be my ex-wife. Now before you start with the "What's wrong? Too possessive to let her go, even in death?" crap let me explain something to you.

It was her fault.

I am not normally a finger-pointer, have no problems accepting fault when it is mine to accept, but in this case it honestly wasn't my idea. I was a prisoner. Shackled to my ex-wife of all people. It was not the stuff of dreams, let me tell you.

Even dead, I could do no right.

Anyway, I'm getting off on a tangent. Thankfully, she found herself a new man and set me loose. But that gets me to problem number three.

Dead or alive a guy still has certain…urges, if you know what I mean. But it's nearly impossible to find a woman who is willing to consider a relationship with a dead guy. Think about it. Have you read any fairy tales where the ghost rides off into the sunset with the princess?

I've made my point.

So here I am, a fella with a five-year boner, looking for a woman with an open mind. She needs to care less about marriage and having babies, you know, the more traditional ideas of a relationship, and care more about finding companionship…and having sex for the sheer enjoyment of it.

Impossible you say? No way. I have one woman in mind, a feisty redhead I lusted after in high school. She was the kind of person who marched to her own tune, so to speak, and I doubt she'll take issue with my dead guy, and thus unmarriageable, status. Since it takes a certain… shall we say, unusual gift…to help me change from spirit to physical form, I'm eager to find her. Shouldn't be too difficult, considering her name…

Chapter One

ဆ

Hope Love Hart cringed at the click on the other end of the phone line. If ever there'd been an angry click, that one had been a furious one.

No doubt about it. That customer would want her money back too, which made three refunds just this week. At this rate, Hope figured she wouldn't make enough money to pay her phone bill this month, let alone her rent.

Hope leaned back in her second-hand office chair with the threadbare seat and sighed. Maybe Mandy, her best friend, a high-school career counselor, had been wrong. What do a bunch of silly questionnaires asking what her favorite color is a zillion different ways say about a person's career options anyway?

She dropped her head. Her forehead hit the desk with a thunk as she mentally sissy-slapped herself. To think she'd left a stable job to follow this pipe dream!

Okay, so her old job had been so boring. Yes, she'd fallen asleep on the job, more than once.

She'd been sick. Both times. Or maybe it had been PMS.

And yes, a job as a receptionist in a sales office that had no foot traffic to speak of, unless you counted the UPS driver, paid peanuts. Barely enough to cover her barest necessities, never mind a few luxuries…like three square meals a day.

So, when Mandy had arrived at Hope's front door, waving a folder in triumph and proclaiming she'd found the perfect solution to Hope's financial worries, Hope had been all ears.

"Dumb, dumb, dumb." She sighed and looked at the clock. Quarter to eleven in the morning. "Whatever made me think I could be a spiritual medium of all things? Sometimes I can't hear real people, sitting right next to me, let alone across dimensions or whatever they're called." She punched a few buttons on her computer to check the status of her most recent eBay purchase, a music CD that was supposed to help the listener get into touch with the spirit world.

A medium who couldn't hear a ghost if it were screaming in her face needed all the help she could get.

She realized the music CD was probably a scam but couldn't resist. While on her beans and rice diet, the price with shipping had almost equated to a week's worth of groceries, she was desperate. Desperate mediums did desperate things.

The computer screen hadn't been updated yet. Evidently her prized purchase was still sitting in a big brown truck, bumping and rumbling down local streets. It would be here soon.

She checked her email, hoping she might have another client requesting an appointment. Her calendar was completely empty for the next several days. Unfortunately, the only email in her box wasn't worth opening. The subject line promised bigger sizes of anatomical parts she didn't possess — darn spam!

Disgusted, and ready to begin the process of finding a real job — to heck with Mandy — she retrieved yesterday's newspaper, which she'd tucked under the couch cushion for safekeeping and skimmed the help wanted ads.

Lots of advertisements for marketing schemes. *Make money! No work!*

Ha, if only!

The doorbell chimed and figuring it had to be the man in brown, she jumped up and charged the door. He was already at the street and halfway back in his truck by the time she got the door open. She found the package sitting on her porch, eagerly snatched it up and slammed the door against the bitterly cold air outside.

Whew! There was one aspect of working at home she would miss—not having to go out in the frigid wasteland that was Metro Detroit in the dead of winter, unless she wanted to of course.

She flopped into her chair and found the nearest sharp instrument—her car key—to cut open the box. It took some effort, but after breaking a sweat as she sawed through the ten layers of tape some sadist had wrapped around the box, she rooted through the pile of foam popcorn to find the plastic jewel case. It wasn't sealed in plastic film or anything. Strange. She could've sworn the listing had said the CD would be brand-new.

Oh well, just less wrapping to fight with.

She flipped open the case, plucked up the CD, which had a solid black label with no lettering whatsoever on it, and slid it into her player. She hit "play".

A shrill whistle blasted from the speakers, then hissing and static. Gosh darn it! The stupid thing was no good!

She turned down the volume then hit the forward button, skipping to song number two, hoping maybe part of the CD would work. When she released the button, she heard the same strange sounds, like the noise you hear when you call a fax line with a telephone.

Shoot!

She hit the eject button and checked the shiny surface for a scratch, found none, then polished it with the bottom of her cotton T-shirt before putting it back in the player. Naturally, she heard the same squealing noise when she hit "play" again.

Pooh. Now she'd have to return it. And she hated returning anything, even library books. Ever the optimist, she left it playing as she dug through the packing materials, hoping to find some instructions.

"Hello, Hope," said a deep, decidedly male voice from behind her as she dumped the foam popcorn on the floor.

The box still in her hands, she spun her chair around and jumped to her feet. "What the he—" The box slipped from her fingers and bounced on the carpet. She felt her eyes bugging out of her head and blinked several times.

That was not a semitransparent man standing in her living room! Nuh-uh!

"Is that the way you always greet your guests?" the man asked.

Was she imagining things or was he getting more…solid? And good-looking?

Wavy dark hair hung to almost his shoulders but it didn't make him look feminine…at all. He had a ruggedly handsome face, with deep hollows under high cheekbones, dark, dark eyes—were they…purple?—a square jaw and a very large, very muscular physique clad in jeans and a white T-shirt.

She took a couple of giant steps backward, bumping into her CD player with her elbow. The CD shut off and like a dream at dawn, the man faded before her eyes until he disappeared completely.

"Ooookaaaay. What was that?" She cautiously approached the spot where the man had been standing and waved her arms through the space. Her left arm sliced through a pocket of ice-cold air and instantly the hairs on it stood on end. She shivered. Little prickles on her nape made her shudder again. "I'm spending too much time trying to talk to the dead. Now I'm imagining things! Need to get out among the living for a while. Either that, or the batch of tea I made last night was spiked with something." She picked up the glass she'd been drinking from and sniffed. Smelled like green tea all right.

Huh.

She slumped into the chair, turned to her computer and looked up the information she'd saved about the CD, hoping she'd find directions on how to return it. Imaginary guy or not, that CD was no good…unless…

Couldn't be!

She skimmed the details of the CD's eBay listing again. On closer examination there was no mention of music, or lectures, or workshops, or any other form of auditory data she'd normally expect to find on a CD. It merely claimed to help bridge the world of the living with the world of the dead.

Maybe it wasn't broken?

Another chill skittered down her back. She turned her head and stared at the player then twisted her neck to look at the empty room behind her. Then, her gaze focused on the exact spot where the man had appeared last time, and her hands shaking, she hit the "play" button again.

The shrill noise made her shivering even worse and she clamped her flattened hands over her aching ears.

"You'll get used to it over time," the deep mellow voice crooned from a different spot, though again, behind her. She spun to the left and glared at the man.

"Would you quit sneaking up on me, you...you ghoul?"

He laughed and it felt like he'd literally reached inside her belly with his hands and tickled her.

She gasped and wrapped her arms around herself. "Glad you think that's so funny because I don't. How are you doing that disappearing-reappearing thing anyway?" Wondering how the screeching racket coming from her player was actually able to make this guy appear, she reached for the power button. "Maybe I should shut this off again to see if—"

He lunged forward and wrapped his long fingers around her wrist. The contact made her gasp and jerk her hand away. A blaze of heat raced up her arm and down to her groin.

She looked up. "What do you think you're doing? No one comes in my house, sneaks up and scares the pants off me and—"

"Really?" He tipped his head, clearly looking below waist level.

"Not literally, you goon. And keep your hands to yourself."

He made a halfhearted attempt at sobering his expression. She could tell he didn't really want to. The left side of his mouth twitched and his eyes sparkled with mischief. Those eyes...so dark. They looked familiar. "Sorry," he said. "I swear I didn't mean to scare you. It just so happened I was standing behind you both times you turned on that machine there. What is it? I've never had such an easy time crossing to the world of the living."

"World of the living? So where, exactly, did you come from? The east side?" she joked, not sure what else one did when faced with a...a strange man who tended to turn transparent from time to time. Of course, in the name of safety, she kept her expression grim, her tone authoritative and aloof.

A girl was a fool if she made nice with every handsome, sexy, yummy guy who happened to materialize out of thin air in her living room.

He laughed. "That's clever. I like you. And in answer to your question, I'm dead."

"Don't I feel special?" she said, trying to maintain her deadpan expression. "I crack a joke and the dead guy likes me now." She shook her head. "Dead. He wants me to believe he's dead."

He grinned, which only made it that much harder to keep her composure. The man could take some serious teasing, that was for sure. A good sport and not too hard on the eyes — he looked like he'd just leapt off the cover of a romance novel. With a bod like that, it might be fun to keep him around a while. Her gaze wandered up and down his form again, taking in every bump and bulge on its way.

Come to think of it, he could use a costume change. Why hadn't she gotten the guy off the cover of a historical romance novel? She'd always liked a hot man in tights. And one of those billowy white shirts that didn't close in the front, so a girl could get a good look at his chest and stomach...

"I came from the place most people call heaven," he said, busting into some very pleasant if not obscene thoughts. "It's actually not really a place in the clouds, though that's a nice way of imagining it. It's more of a different state."

"Interesting. Different state, eh? Like Ohio?"

"No, like...well, it's hard to explain. Did you ever take physics in school? Oh...no, I remember now."

"So you're trying to tell me you're dead?" Not really letting his last comment register, she circled him like he was the latest Mercedes model, checking out the tires, bumpers, body...Nice shoulders, tight abs, small waist, narrow hips, long legs that seemed to go on forever...cute, round butt. She sucked in a sigh and rounded his left side, halting in front of him again.

"Exactly." He nodded enthusiastically. "That's right. Dead."

"You look good for a dead guy." She took a second peek at his butt. That was really nice...

His chest puffed up with pride. "Thanks. I work out."

She straightened up and gave her voice the authoritative edge it had somehow lost. "Now don't let my little comment go to your head. I just meant there isn't a hint of decay on you anywhere. Course, I can't see your toes. I'd imagine your toes would be the first to go, considering the lack of circulation and all."

"Of course there isn't. My toes are fine. This isn't my body."

"Ew!" She took a giant step backward "Whose is it then? Did you borrow it from somewhere? Oh God. If you did, I really don't want to know where you found it or what happened to the poor guy you took it from."

"No, no, no! I mean, it's my body. This is what I looked like in life. But it's not my permanent body. It's my spirit in another form, a more solid form."

"You can say that again," she murmured under her breath.

"What'd you say?" he asked.

"Oh, nothing." She coughed. "I just said…solid form. Yes, I understand. Like steam compared to…er, ice, right?" *I could use a block of ice right about now. Anything to chill me out.*

"Yes!" His face lit. "That's right. No offense, but you're a lot smarter than I gave you credit for in high school."

"Wait a minute! That's the second time you've hinted that I know you from high school. Do I know you? That was…" she coughed again, "…a few years ago."

"Yes. Class of '90."

"You're kidding." She squinted her eyes because for some reason she could see better that way—even though she'd never needed glasses in her life and had perfect twenty-twenty vision—and really scrutinized his features. No way. She'd never gone to school with such a drop-dead gorgeous hunk. She'd remember a guy who looked like this. No doubt about it. "You're lying."

"Am not." He crossed his thick arms over his chest. His biceps bulged. Yummy.

"Oh yeah? What school did I go to?" she challenged, watching his eyes. Somewhere she'd heard when someone was lying to you, they looked to the left and if they were trying to remember something, they looked to the right.

He looked down and to the right. "Canton."

Maybe she had it wrong. Maybe they looked to the right when they were lying. She could never remember those kinds of handy facts when she needed them. "Oh yeah, well, maybe you just got your hands on someone else's yearbook."

"Do you honestly know anyone who still has their high-school yearbooks?"

"Yes. I do."

"Good! I'll show you then. My name's Jeremy. Jeremy Burbank."

"Jeremy Burbank…" she repeated, as if saying his name might jog her memory. She shook her head. "I'm getting nothing."

"We were in English nine together. And speech. And American history. And health…"

"We took that many classes together and I don't remember you?"

"Well, I did look a little different then."

That admission was enough to make her lunge toward the bookcase to find her high-school yearbook. She had to know who this guy was, dead or not.

"If you were in my English class, you must've been in my graduating class, right?" Finding her senior yearbook, she plopped into her office chair and started flipping through the pages.

"Yup." He rested his rear end on the arm of her chair, mere inches from her elbow. He leaned closer, his chest so close to her shoulder it wouldn't take more than a slight shift in her position to touch it. His breath warmed her exposed neck, thanks to her hair being swept up in a clip.

She shivered.

"Cold?" he asked.

She nodded and leaned a bit to the left.

Being a male, and obviously enjoying what he was doing to her, he leaned too. She moved. He moved. And on it went until she was practically horizontal on top of her desk, dizzy, breathless, and ready to jump his dead guy bones.

Fed up with his game, she nudged him with her elbow. "Okay, Romeo, back off," she said, sounding a whole lot tougher than she felt.

He shifted to the right, but not enough to make her lungs work properly. Or her eyes. She was kind of staring through the pages, not looking at them.

Trying like heck to comprehend what was on the glossy white paper, she flipped pages with her cold fingers. Her palms were sweaty, her heart thumping in her ear. She'd been this close to many a man, but never had she reacted like this, like she hadn't had sex in decades.

Of course, none of them had ever claimed to be dead, either. And it didn't help that she hadn't had sex in a long, long time. Not decades, but over a year.

She stopped on the page with Bs. She'd chosen her senior yearbook because the pictures of her classmates would be larger. And considering the fact that she was so flustered she would probably fail to recognize herself at the moment, she figured the bigger the picture the better.

"Barns…Boyle…" she read aloud, running her fingertip under each row of pictures. "Burbank." She stopped then looked at the picture. The face she saw in that photograph looked nothing like the one hovering over her shoulder. "Ha. Liar. I remember him. Super shy. Quiet.

Nerdy. Hardly said two words our whole senior year. That," she said, stabbing a finger at the picture, "is not you."

"Look closely. I ditched the braces. Gained a few — oh seventy pounds or so," he said in her ear, which made her shiver again, for an entirely different reason. "Learned to talk to women."

She tried to look past the sharply angled face, pointed chin and mouthful of metal that was a seventeen-year-old Jeremy Burbank, to the man he would become.

If he gained some weight, his bones thickening with age, he just might...he could very well...

Okay. It was him.

"Talk about a change," she said, her gaze ping-ponging between the man and the book. "And I'm not just talking about physical, although that part is quite... noteworthy."

"Yeah. Fifteen years in a gym'll do that for a guy."

"Then I'm all for the gym," she quipped as she shut the book and pushed it aside. "Anyway, now that we've determined that this is a high-school reunion of sorts, don't you think you should be going home — or heaven, or wherever — now? I mean, it's been fun and all that but I wonder what the purpose of this visit is?"

"You'll have to tell me that, beautiful. You're the one with the machine that made me become physical again."

"In my defense, I didn't know it would call an old friend from high-school."

"Friend? We were friends?" He grinned.

"Okay, okay. I was one of the freaks and you were one of the geeks. I didn't give you the time of day. But still, I didn't do this on purpose. I bought that CD to help me with my job."

"Job? What are you doing these days?"

"Psychic medium," she answered with a nod. "Unfortunately, there was one small fact I ignored when I decided to quit my regular paying day job to give it a try."

"What's that?"

"I'm not psychic."

He laughed. The low rumble hit her deep in the belly again. It felt like a bunch of happy bubbles that stirred laughter inside her too.

She giggled and met his gaze. "Only I would do something so stupid."

"I wouldn't call it stupid. I'd call it brilliant."

"Oh yeah? Why's that?"

"Simple." He stood up, nudged her chair until it had turned slightly and her knees were wedged between his thighs and then he rested his hands on the armrests and lowered his head until he was practically nose to nose with her. Her throat squeezed shut, trapping the used air in her lungs and fresh air out. "Your skill level as a psychic just went from novice to professional. After all, whether you want to accept it or not, you've spent the last twenty minutes flirting with a dead guy." He tipped his head and slowly lowered it.

Oh God, the dead guy's going to kiss me!

A gasp slipped through her slightly parted lips.

Chapter Two

മ

Jeremy stifled a moan as he stared at Hope's full ruby-hued lips. Her breath smelled sweet. Her lush mouth silently tempted him to take a taste, just one shy swipe of his tongue. Yet he resisted just before his mouth made contact with hers. It was too soon. She wasn't ready.

Pushing Hope Hart definitely wasn't in his best interest at the moment. He was too vulnerable, at her mercy. If she flipped that switch again, he'd be gone. And he had no idea if he'd have the strength to come back. His experience with changing was limited.

Very limited. Like this was the first time he'd actually succeeded. And he'd tried before. Plenty of times.

With slight pressure on the arms of her chair, he pushed himself away. Once again fully erect—in more than one sense—he smiled down at her, waiting for her to shake off the shock. He knew it wouldn't take long, had the feeling Hope didn't lose control of her actions, or reactions, easily or for long.

Within a heartbeat, he saw the glint of control spark in her eye again. Yep. She was back and ready for more.

"So, I wonder…how many of your dead friends did you bring with you?" she said as she scooted the chair back a few feet in an obvious attempt to put more distance between them. He didn't try to get near her again. He'd allow her her space.

For now.

Besides, at the moment, he needed a little space of his own. The erection pressing urgently at his shorts was causing some major discomfort. His balls were tight too. All in all, he was feeling just shy of miserable. He turned, made a show of searching the room behind him then looked at her again. "None, evidently. You don't see any, do you?"

"Glad to hear that," she said with a sarcastic edge in her voice. He could tell she wasn't completely sold on his dead guy routine, which in all fairness he couldn't blame her for doubting. If the tables were turned, he probably wouldn't believe it either.

"But I thought the whole idea of being a medium was to communicate with the dead," he pointed out as he took the opportunity to wander around the room, check out the pictures on the fireplace mantel. Not a single one with a man or kids, he noted, rather belatedly. While she'd said in health class she never wanted to be married, he had to accept her attitude could've changed over the years.

"It is. But talking to one dead person at a time is enough for me. Give me a break. I'm still getting used to the idea."

"Take all the time you need." He picked up a nice snapshot of her standing on a mountaintop somewhere. The gray-blue tops of the craggy mountains were covered in snow. She looked beautiful, a few scarlet tendrils blown across her cheek, her eyes glittering with life. "Done some traveling, I see."

"A little."

She stood and crossed the room. As she stepped nearer, his entire body acknowledged her closeness. His nose filled with her sweet scent and his nerves tingled.

"Can we quit talking about me and talk about you for a minute?" She swiped the picture from him and set it back in its place.

"Gladly. I'm a guy. I like to talk about myself. What'd you want to know?"

"How about how long ago you died, for starters. Was it a long, long time ago? Oh! Oh! I have to ask, when you died did you learn about your past lives? Did you reincarnate from like the Renaissance or something interesting? I've always wondered about that past life-reincarnation thing."

"Nope. 'Fraid not. I died about five years ago...for the first and only time."

"Newly dead, then. And not able to give me any obscure historical facts that'll earn me a Nobel Prize."

He shrugged. "Sorry."

"So what are you doing here then? Are you here to help me see the error of my ways like Clarence in *It's a Wonderful Life*?"

"No, not really. Looks like you're doing fine to me."

"Huh. Oh, maybe you're here to protect me? Am I about to be murdered or something?"

"No, not that I know of. But I would protect you if it came to that."

She screwed her pretty face into an expression of confusion. "In the movies there's always a reason why a dead guys shows up in a person's living room." Her eyes widened with alarm. "Oh, you're not a bad dead guy, gonna drag me down to hell or anything are you?"

"Heck no! Hate the place. Wouldn't want to live there. Wouldn't want to see you go there either."

"Then what are you doing here?" she asked, tossing her hands in the air.

He lifted his arms and shrugged his shoulders in the universal sign of I-don't-have-a-frickin'-clue and then guessed, "Seducing you?"

That earned him a belly-busting guffaw from his intended seducee. Then she took a few steps away from him. Tears wetting her eyes, she said between sputtering chuckles, "You? A dead guy? Want to seduce me? That's just plain...creepy."

"Creepy? No woman's ever called me creepy before."

"Well, that's probably because you never tried to pick one up after you were dead." She emphasized that last word.

"You have a point. You really think it's so bad though? I mean, you haven't given me a chance to tell you all the advantages of sleeping with a dead guy."

"I don't think I want to hear this."

"Try me."

"Okay, stud." She sat in her chair and crossed both her arms and legs. "Go ahead."

If there was one thing Jeremy had learned during his brief but explosive marriage to Stephanie, his ex-wife, it was that a woman who crossed both arms and legs while claiming to listen to him had no intention of hearing a word.

So either he was a glutton for punishment or just plain stubborn because he had no intention of backing down. Hope's mind might be locked tight as a bank vault, but he'd find the key. "First, you don't have to worry about birth control because I can't get you knocked up."

"Not a worry. I'm on the Depo shot."

Undeterred, he continued, "Second, you don't have to worry about diseases because I can't carry them or pass them to you."

"Isn't that romantic? 'Sleep with me. I can't give you a disease.' Sorry, but I've heard that line before, and it didn't come from a corpse. You'll have to try harder."

"Okay." Obviously the logical approach he had been so sure would work was failing him. But what would work better? If he had his druthers, he'd walk over to her, throw her over his shoulder and take her into the bedroom where he could show her.

That would convince her for sure, if she didn't shut off the machine that kept him there first. He wasn't willing to risk it.

"Third, you don't have to worry about me asking for more than just sex, like marriage or anything, because I can't," he said.

He caught a slight glint in her eye. By golly that one caught her attention.

"No threats to drag me down the aisle?" she asked, one eyebrow lifted.

"Not unless it's a store aisle, assuming I can even leave this room. I'm not sure about that one yet."

"No demands that I spend every waking moment with you?" One corner of her mouth lifted in a lopsided smile.

"You control when I come and go," he admitted, pointing at the CD player. "It's up to you when I leave. I didn't want to tell you this but if you turn the machine off I'll go back to being a spirit again. I don't have the strength to change on my own, or even stay this way after I've changed. I'm at your mercy. Completely."

"It sucks to be you then." Despite her strong words, she looked very pleased with what she was hearing. She reached toward the player, a playful sparkle in her emerald eyes. "Maybe I should put it to the test."

"Please." He wanted to lunge forward but didn't, fearing she'd punch the button in reaction. He just held up his hands. "All fun and games aside, you should understand that I don't know if I'll be able to come back once you shut that thing off."

"You have twice already."

"I know. But I happened to be the closest spirit to you at the moment. That might not always be the case."

Her eyes widened with understanding. "You mean there are others? Here? Now?" He adored her when she looked like that. So vulnerable and innocent, in complete contrast to her normal demeanor.

"We're — I mean, they're — around you all the time." Taking advantage of her discomfort, he closed the distance between them, reaching for her arms. His skin barely making contact with the material of her shirtsleeves, he ran his hands down her arms and let them rest on top of her hands, which were sitting restlessly on her lap. His palms on top of the backs of her hands, he twined his fingers through hers.

"They can see me?" she whispered.

"Yes, they can."

"How many are there here now?" Her head swiveled side to side on the narrow column of her neck. A red curl dropped from the clip holding her hair on top of her head to rest on the swell of her breast. It taunted him, calling for his touch but he resisted yet again.

No doubt about it, this woman would test his self-control. Independent to a fault, she'd insist he give her space or shut him out forever. He couldn't live with that thought.

"When I'm on this side with you I can't see them either," he explained. He rubbed her thumb with his.

She wriggled her hands out from under his. "What about before? Before I turned that noise on? You could see them then. Right?"

"Yes. There were a lot of spirits here. Probably a couple dozen in this room alone."

She gasped. "That many?" He saw her shiver and lifted his hands to her shoulders. "You said you hadn't brought any of your dead friends with you, remember?"

"Yeah, well, I didn't bring them to this side. And they aren't my friends. I don't know who they are. Can't say I've ever seen so many in a single room before. You must be a better psychic than you thought. The spirits are here. You just couldn't hear them."

"Until now."

"Yeah."

He saw her tremble and ached to ease her fears.

"Wow. This has been so weird, this conversation, this whole day." Her gaze swept the room. Back and forth, back and forth, like she was searching for something. "I'm not sure how I think about it. Parts of it sound great."

"Maybe you should just focus on those parts for now. Let the rest settle in when it will."

"Yeah." Her gaze found his. "You were nearest. Why?"

"That's simple. I've been hoping for a chance to talk to you. I've spent nights whispering in your ears when you're sleeping. When you're dreaming your spirit is more attuned to our vibrations."

She tucked her hair behind her ear and touched her earlobe. "You talked to me?"

"Yeah. I never expected to get a chance like this, to touch you, smell you. Have you see me too."

"But why? Why me?"

He kneeled before her and took her right hand in his. Before he spoke, he inhaled deeply, catching the floral scent clinging to her clothes. "Because in all these years I've never been able to forget about you," he admitted, knowing it would either seal his doom or reassure her. "When I was living, I wasn't given the chance to tell you how I felt."

Breathless, his cock pushing urgently against the front of his jeans, he waited for her to respond.

"Great, now I don't just have live guys giving me a line to get in my pants. I have dead guys doing it too." Hiding the want pulsing through her body with every stuttering, irregular heartbeat, she put up her usual take-no-nonsense front. Truth be told, his confession had practically melted the frigid ice that had encased her heart for ages. Almost. It was still a long way off from being completely thawed, thank goodness.

Where would a girl be if not for her protective ice shield?

To think this guy had gone to such lengths to find her, even after he was dead. She swallowed a sigh. It was the stuff of a movie. Totally romantic. Kind of reminded her of *Ghost*, a classic film and one of her all-time favorites.

She resisted the urge to fall into his arms and let him have his way with her and instead thought about how to keep him around for a while without giving up everything—her freedom, her heart.

Her mind wrapped around an idea. "Is there a way you can help me with my job?"

"Probably not in this form, in the physical. Like I said, I can't see or hear the spirits any better than you can when I'm on this side."

"What if we set up some sort of system? You go back, gather the information I need, then return a set time later?"

"I'd be your spiritual delivery boy?"

"Yeah. Delivery boy." She watched as he considered her proposal for a moment.

"What'll I get out of the deal? You realize you're asking for a lot," he said. "I'll have to track down the spirit you want to contact then convince them to give whatever information you're looking for, then cross back over to the physical. That crossing over part is no fun. Let me tell you. It hurts like hell."

She could see what he was doing, presenting his hardships, building his case. He wanted something from her. "What'll it cost me?"

"Hmmm…" He twisted his lips as he thought. "Your nights."

"Huh?"

"You'll have to spend your nights with me if you want me to spend my days playing glorified telegraph courier for you."

Yeah. Typical guy. Naming sex as his price.

She shook her head. "No way. I don't think so. I've got too much pride to do that."

"You'd turn down the chance to possibly become the most well-known and respected physic medium in the world because of a little pride?"

"It's all I've got. I'm not going to let you—dead or not—coerce me into bed. That's weak." She poked him in the chest. "I've never—never!—paid a man sex to get ahead in my life and I never will."

"You know what they say about never saying never."

"Ha!" Just because she could, she repeated it again, "I will never give a man sex to get ahead in life."

"Give or receive? You might just like it, you know." He stepped closer, and sitting, she was forced to tilt her head back to look at his face. His hands landed on her shoulders and his fingers started working the stiff muscles. The gentle kneading felt great. "You have to admit you're a little tense. Some sex might be the cure—"

Her eyelids fell shut as he continued to rub. "Yeah, yeah. I get laid and all my woes'll disappear. Tell me another one."

"Okay. What if I sweeten the deal?" he added, his fingertips walking down her arms. "Give me a chance to prove I'm not just a guy out to take advantage of you."

She inhaled a slow, deep breath, catching the scent of his tangy cologne. "How're you going to do that? I mean, it's already pretty darn clear what you're up to, dead guy."

"Simple. You'll still spend your nights with me, but we won't do anything you don't want to and we won't...you know..." his eyes glittered devilishly, "...do the horizontal mambo until you tell me we can. I'll just give you pleasure..." He leaned so close his breath tickled her ear. "...in any way I see fit."

That sounded pretty darn tempting. Anticipation zigzagged up her spine. "Like...how?"

"Oh, I don't know." He brushed something along her chin. A fingertip? His lips? She drew in a sharp breath. "Massages, candlelit dinners..."

"...taking out the trash, fixing the occasional plugged toilet," she continued in a whisper.

"That wasn't the direction I was heading but it's your fantasy, baby." He emphasized fantasy. She felt him back away and had to force her arms to stay at her sides, knowing if she didn't, she'd grab any part of him she could reach and yank him back. She wanted him close. Wanted to feel his breath warm her neck, wanted to taste his mouth, wanted his hands exploring her body.

He said, "If that'll make you happy, I'm all for it. Though I should warn you, when it comes to electrical stuff, forget it. I'm more of a danger than a help."

"My fantasy...I like that," she practically moaned. Hearing the hunger in her own voice, and not happy at herself for exposing it, she cleared her throat and said in a stronger tone, "And thanks for the warning about the electrical stuff. I'll definitely keep that in mind." Before she gave herself too long to think about it, and talk herself out of it, she opened her eyes and thrust her hand forward. "You, dead guy, have a deal."

"Good."

And she shook hands with Jeremy Burbank, hoping she hadn't just made a pact with the devil himself.

That sly grin on his face sure suggested otherwise, that and the fact that all the way around it seemed like she was the only one who had anything to gain from the deal.

Generally speaking, that usually meant the opposite — that she had everything to lose.

Chapter Three

ဆာ

"So, when do we begin?" Hope said, anxious to get started—at least on her part of the deal. Then again, his supposed part sounded like a winner too. A shoulder rub and a meal that didn't come out of a box was sounding pretty darn nice.

"Right now, I guess," he answered, not looking particularly pleased. He rested his cute butt on the edge of her desk.

"What's wrong? You got what you wanted."

"I'm just not sure how this crossing to and fro is going to work out. You could catch the wrong spirit and end up with a big surprise. Although the real evil spirits aren't allowed to roam loose—"

"Where do they go?" she interrupted, suddenly not so sure this was such a great idea.

"The ones that are thoroughly evil and cannot be trusted to travel freely among the others are condemned to the place you call hell…eventually."

"Oh." She nodded. "So it's kind of like the afterlife's version of prison."

"Yeah, with no chance of parole."

"But at least it protects the other spirits, right? And people too."

"Sometimes but not always, from what I hear. They are given a certain length of time first, before their trial."

"A certain length of time? I don't like the sound of that." She wrapped herself in her own arms and shrugged, wondering how comforting and warm it would be wrapped in Jeremy's thick arms instead. "How can we make sure I don't invite a bad guy into my living room?" she asked.

"We'll have to set up a system, but understand there's still no guarantee you'll get me every time you turn that thing on."

A heavy lump settled in her gut. "Okay. But I can just turn it off and they'll go away. Right?"

"I don't know."

"Oh." Now she really questioned whether this was such a good idea. She could end up living like those people in that *Poltergeist* movie. Trees turning into demons. Skeletons in the swimming pool. Good thing she didn't like to swim.

"So, what's my first assignment?"

She turned to her computer and pulled up her next appointment. "Mrs. Evaline Drummand. She's a regular. Her husband passed away very suddenly about six months ago and she's been trying to reach him. I'm not sure exactly why, whether she just misses him or more. His name was George. That's all I know. Think you can find him?"

"You have an address?"

"Yes, 1443 Whittaker."

"I'll do my best." He glanced at the clock. He leaned low, his chest pressing against her shoulder, to pull a piece of blank paper from the printer. "Pen?"

She pulled one from a box she kept in the drawer and watched as he scribbled down a short shopping list.

When he was finished, he straightened up, folded the paper and handed it to her. "Make sure you have these things for tonight and don't turn on that thing until seven on the dot. Okay?"

"Okay."

"Now, hit the button. I'm going back to find George Drummand."

Unfolding the note, her face heated as she read the first item on the list—handcuffs. She looked at Jeremy's face, caught the wicked glimmer in his eyes...and pushed the button.

The last thing to fade from sight was that evil grin. It didn't fade from her memory near as quick, and not without causing some serious damage to her willpower.

* * * * *

At exactly 6:59, Hope sat at her desk, finger on the play button of her CD player, and watched the second hand on her clock. Outside of going to the bank to cash in a savings bond she'd gotten from her grandmother ages ago, getting the shopping done, taking a shower and shaving parts of her body that hadn't seen a razor in who knows how long—not that she expected him to see any of them—she hadn't gotten a single thing accomplished today.

It was all his fault, darned sexy dead guy. He was evil! Evil, and tempting, and funny, and...and...all kinds of interesting parts of her body warmed as she imagined his face as she'd last seen it. That crooked, bad-boy smile, the crinkles at the corners of his eyes. Shoot! She had a serious case of lust for the guy. Already.

Ten seconds, nine, eight, seven...

She had to fortify her defenses. No time to be weak…

Five, four, three, two…

Oh boy. Here goes! She closed her eyes, scrunched up her shoulders, like that would protect her from anything if she summoned an evil ghost, and hit "play".

"Hi baby."

Jeremy! Thank God! "Hey dead guy, how'd it go?"

"I found the bastard."

"Isn't it unkind to talk ill of the dead?"

"This guy deserves it. It's no wonder his wife kept coming to you for help. He took all their money out of their joint account and hid it in an account in his name only. Then he watched her struggle for the last six months, knowing the money might eventually end up in the state's coffers."

"Really? That's not the type of man his wife had described to me."

"She's probably too ashamed to tell you the truth, or in denial. But take my word for it, he's as cold as they come."

"Poor Mrs. Drummand!" A sharp needle of guilt pricked her for all the money she'd collected from the desperate woman.

"I got the bank name, address and account number. She should be able to claim the money now." He held out his hand and, not exactly sure what he was looking for, she set her hand in his. He squeezed it and smiled. "This is nice but can I have something to write with? I want to write down the information before I forget."

"Oh! Of course!" Her cheeks instantly flaming, she yanked her hand away and gathered a pen and piece of paper. She studied his profile as he bent over and wrote the name and address of the bank and account number. He scooted it across the smooth desk until it was sitting smack-dab in front of her. "This is great. I'll call her tomorrow and give it to her." She looked in his eyes. "Thanks. You really did something good here."

"My pleasure." He slapped his hands together and then rubbed them. "And speaking of pleasure, I'm off to the kitchen to whip up some chicken. You bought all the ingredients I asked for, right?" He strolled across the living room toward the kitchen and she hopped up to follow him.

"Everything but the handcuffs. Krogers was all sold out of those."

"A shame. My Chicken Marseilles just isn't the same without them." He flipped on the kitchen light, gathered the ingredients from the fridge and spread them out on the counter. Then he went about preparing the food. The man chopped and sautéed like one of those guys on the Food Network.

Doing her best to stay out of his way, she sat at the snack bar on a swivel stool and rested her chin on her fists. In no time the kitchen was full of the tantalizing scents of garlic and grilled chicken. "So, were you a chef...before?"

"No. Just married to a woman who hated to cook."

"I'm not much of a cook either," she confessed. "But I sure like to eat."

"Nothing wrong with that. My mother, who was married to a man who thought it was sacrilege to step foot in a kitchen, decided her sons would never have that attitude. So she sent us all to cooking school for two years. Both my older brothers ended up becoming chefs."

"Both?"

"Yeah. Mom and Dad Burbank had three boys. I'm the baby."

"How'd your father take two of his boys becoming cooks?"

"Chefs," Jeremy corrected. "Not good. He blustered his way into a heart attack after Sam—that's the second one—told him he was not only going to be a chef but he was also gay."

"Oh my."

Jeremy flipped the contents of the fry pan with a flick of his wrist then stirred some sauce he had simmering in a pot. It was something watching a man who was so large and strong and dangerous-looking doing a Betty Crocker routine. "He never got to find out what I was going to be."

"Which was?"

"A cop, just like the old man."

"Daddy's boy became a policeman. He would've been proud."

"Yeah." He lifted his strong arms, making biceps and shoulder muscles bunch and bulge as he searched the cupboards. Not exactly eager to see him stop looking, she didn't help him in his search. Eventually he found the dishes and set two on the counter.

He filled them both with chicken, noodles and vegetables then carried them to the set table. Hope lit the candles, set a bottle of wine on the table, along with two empty glasses, and took her seat.

He picked up the bottle. "What kind of wine did you get?"

"You just said white. Didn't mention anything specific, so I bought the first bottle that looked decent. I'm not much of a wine drinker, honestly. I'd rather go for a nice cold diet cola."

"Not with this meal you won't." The neck of the bottle in one big fist, he went to the kitchen and rummaged through her drawers, no doubt looking for a corkscrew.

"Check the one nearest the stove," she suggested.

"Got it. Thanks." He returned, opened the bottle, which was a sight, considering the muscles that were required to twist a corkscrew—she'd never noticed that little detail before—then filled both glasses. He sat and lifted his glass. "A toast?"

"Okay." She lifted hers.

"To evenings."

She chuckled. "That's it?"

"Yeah. I'm a man of few words."

"Could've fooled me," she teased as she touched the rim of her glass to his. Her gaze tangled with his, much like the twisted, knotted angel-hair pasta on her plate, she hazarded a small sip. It wasn't bad, much smoother than she expected. The second swallow went down even easier.

The wine's sweet flavor lingering, she took a bite of the pasta. Her taste buds came to life, shocked from a coma-like state they'd evidently been lulled into by months—no, years—of bland, prepared foods. She closed her eyes and savored the flavors doing the cha-cha on her tongue. She sighed.

"You like? It's among my specialties."

"Among? As in you have more than one?" she asked, not attempting to hide the appreciation in her voice. She opened her eyes and found his gaze hadn't left her face.

"I'd like to think so, yes." He forked a piece of chicken into his mouth and she watched as it slipped between his lips. A tiny drip of sauce clung to his lower lip and she nearly jumped out of her chair to lick it away.

"Then I can't wait to try them all," she heard herself say.

"Me neither," he said in a low voice that suggested they weren't talking about food any longer. An undercurrent of challenge rumbled in that deep baritone of his. She couldn't miss it.

Despite the fact that she'd always prided herself on never backing down from a challenge, her gaze dropped like a lead balloon from his face. His expression had been so hot, so tempting, so intense. It had made her insides feel all squiggly. Like a bucket full of unearthed night crawlers. It wasn't a particularly pleasant feeling.

Her gaze focused on her plate, she decided to appease her skittering innards with lots of chicken and noodles... and some more of that wine. He'd been right about that. The flavors blended perfectly. The dinner wouldn't have been the same with a diet cola.

Thankfully, her hunky ghost friend took her cue and let her appease her jittery insides with as much food and wine as she dared. But she knew he was watching her. Steady waves of awareness zipped over the top of her head and down her spine every so often, which made her squirm in her chair.

Finally, her plate empty, her glass empty, she looked up and caught a friendly smile.

"Did you enjoy your dinner?" he asked.

"Very much."

"Excellent." He stood, stacked her plate on top of his, scooped up both empty glasses and took the whole shebang to the kitchen. Feeling like she should be doing something besides sitting on her rump, she followed him.

"Shouldn't I be doing that? I mean, you cooked…" Her sentence trailed off as he set the dish he'd been rinsing in the sink and shut off the running water. There was a glint in his eye as he took one, two, three steps toward her.

"Oh, don't worry. Your time is coming," he murmured.

"What's that mean?"

"Well, you didn't expect me to do all this—" he traced a fingertip along the neckline of her top, leaving a blaze of singed nerve endings over her chest, "—without benefiting somehow. Did you?"

A lump the size of Mount Saint Helens formed in her throat as dread and anticipation shot through her body like a bolt of lightning. She coughed violently, her face hot.

He scooped up the wineglass and turning, filled it with cold water from the tap. His fingers brushed hers as he handed her the glass.

She guzzled the water then set the glass on the counter with a delicate clink.

"Okay?" he asked. His brows were scrunched together in worry.

"Fine," she croaked. She coughed then added, "I'm just not feeling myself tonight. Must be the wine."

He nodded with understanding then took her hand in his.

She smiled inwardly at the way her small hand felt in his much bigger one. His grip was warm and gentle as he led her to the living room couch. Thankful for the support, since her legs suddenly felt as soft as melted ice cream, she didn't hesitate to sit. He sat next to her then twisted his upper body to face her.

She stared at his cotton-covered kneecap. Although his knees were very nice, staring at them was slightly less intimidating than staring at his gorgeous mug. He was wearing black pants. A sharp crease cut down the front of each leg. "Nice pants," she commented absentmindedly.

"Thanks."

"I...er, didn't know a ghost could change clothes." She wasn't surprised when he used an index finger placed strategically at the point of her chin to coax her to look up.

Thankfully, his gaze had cooled from lava-hot-wicked to simmering-erotic. It was a slight improvement. At least she was able to look at him and breathe regularly at the same time now.

He moistened those adorable lips of his with the tip of his tongue before he spoke. "I know this whole dead guy thing has got to be weird but I want you to try to forget about the fact that I'm dead, okay?"

She nodded mutely, not bothering to explain that she had indeed forgotten he was dead. The state of her nerves had nothing to do with his non-alive status, at least at the moment.

"Can you do that for me? Forget that I'm dead?" he asked, shifting his position so his upper body was closer. The scent of his cologne tickled her nose.

"Sure. It might help if you didn't repeat it over and over."

He chuckled. His amazingly deep bluish-purple eyes—like grape juice—sparkled and she couldn't help staring at them. "Fair enough. I promise I won't mention that I'm d—"

"Don't say it!" Her hand shot out to his mouth and she pressed her index finger against his lips. She was sorry she'd done that within a heartbeat.

Clearly taking advantage of the proximity between her fingertip and his mouth, he pursed his lips and then drew her finger into the wet warmth of his mouth. His tongue curled around the bottom of it as he gently suckled.

Her face hot, she yanked her hand away and scolded, "You're bad! I can't believe you just did that."

He looked very pleased with himself as he said, "Thank you. I try."

For that, he got a smack in the gut. Not a hard one, just a playful one. Naturally, he overreacted, doubling over and howling like she'd punched him with all her might.

The tension broken, at least for the moment, she enjoyed the laughter they shared. When it died down to stifled giggles, she said, "It was actually the comment about what you wanted to get out of this deal that had me scared. I knew it was too good to be true, you playing male indentured servant for nothing. I mean, you said no sex. Remember?"

"I'm not asking for much," he answered, his eyes wide with forced innocence. He blinked a few times, evidently trying to drive home the trust-me-I'm-innocent thing. Of course, she wasn't buying it.

"Oh yeah?" she asked.

"Sure." He gave her a single nod. "I'll cook for you, clean for you, serve your every need. In return, I want only one thing from you."

"And that would be?" she urged, knowing she was about to be sucker-punched but not sure which part to protect.

He leaned even closer and drilled her with his gaze. "I want you to share your every fantasy with me," he whispered.

Her face heated for a split second and then she retorted, "Oh, that's easy. You're already playing it out. I've always dreamed of having a man serve my every request. Only one thing, though. I've always imagined he'd be wearing a G-string."

He grinned. "No, that's not what I meant. I want you to share your sexual fantasies with me."

"Oh." The mountain in her throat was back. Although it was now the size of Mt. Everest. She tried to jump up to escape to the kitchen for a cold drink to cool her heated insides, but Jeremy caught her wrist and gave it a gentle but firm yank, sending her right back into her seat...next to him.

"Uh-uh. You're not running away from me now."

A little angry and a lot flustered, she shoved at his rock-hard chest. It was one heck of a nice chest. It took more self-control than she thought she possessed to keep from leaning up against that wide bulk and purring like a content kitty. "Back off, buddy. I was just getting a drink."

"In a minute. I want to talk about this first."

"No, now. Quit being so controlling. This is my house. I should be able to get a drink any time I damn well want to."

"Sure. But every time I try to talk about anything serious with you, you hide from me. Why?"

"Because…" She couldn't think of a good reason so she didn't finish her explanation, just left that single word hanging there all by itself.

"You see? This surprises me." He traced her jawline with his thumb. His fingers curled around the back of her neck. "After the way you were in high school, I wouldn't have expected you to be such a shrinking violet about anything, including sex."

She let his words sink in then stammered, "I…don't know how to take that. Are you suggesting I was a whore? Because I wasn't, thank you very much."

"Oh no, baby. That's not what I meant at all." Seemingly trying to appease her rankled nerves, he kneaded the knotted muscles at the base of her neck with strong fingers. "You were sexy, but in an understated way. I could tell you weren't trying to be sexy, like some of the girls were. That's why I found you so irresistible."

His reminder of their semi-shared past soothed her a bit, that and the magic he was performing with his fingers.

Wow, she had no idea how tight her neck had been. She let her head fall forward until her chin rested against her breastbone.

"That's it," he said. "I won't push you. But I want you to share more with me than your dirty toilet." With his hands on her shoulders, he gently coaxed her to turn so her back was to him. He went to work massaging away the tension in her neck and shoulders as he added, "It's the least you could do. Satisfy a guy's curiosity. It's not like I'm going to tell anyone."

"True," she agreed, feeling herself relax, thanks to his skillful manipulation of muscles, tendons and skin.

"Just remember, I won't ever force you to do something you don't want to do. I promise. If you just want to tell me about them that's fine. We don't have to act them out if you don't want to."

"Act them out?" She felt herself slumping forward. Whether from the wine or the massage, she was becoming very relaxed.

He stood and helped her lie down on her stomach. She buried her face in the couch cushions and enjoyed the massage. Slowly he worked out the kinks in her shoulders then moved down her back until he was obliterating the knots at the base of her spine, just above the low-rise waist of her jeans.

As his touches became lighter, less like a massage and more like a caress, heat started to pool between her legs. She let out a muffled moan which didn't stop him. A teasing fingertip slipped under the gaping waist of her jeans, tickling the sensitive spot just above her crack. A quiver shimmied up her spine and a blaze shot to her pussy. Hot and cold at the same time, she groaned and wriggled, tipping her hips slightly to put pressure on her mound.

"So what do you say?"

"Huh?" she asked, not sure what he was asking about. She felt him drawing nearer.

His chest grazed her back. "Tell me your fantasy," he whispered in her ear. "Just one. Maybe your very first fantasy." He backed away and resumed rubbing her back through her clothing. Like that would make this any easier. Hah!

She drew in a deep breath and tried to remember her very first fantasy. "I guess it was along the lines of a big, sexy man saving me...I uh, used to watch *Emergency*. I thought that dark-haired guy was such a fox. I was just a kid then...I'd fall asleep imagining him scooping me into his strong arms and carrying me out of a fire, or flood, or some other natural disaster." She could feel the heat of an embarrassed blush on her cheeks. "Of course, that wasn't really a sexual fantasy. I didn't have sex with him in my daydreams."

"Thank you." He pressed a kiss to the back of her neck and goose bumps popped up all over her upper body. "Now, you get a reward."

"You mean the massage wasn't my reward?"

"Heck no. That was just a warm-up." He jumped up, leaving her to lift her swimmy head to see where he was off to in such a hurry.

"You did buy the whipped cream I asked for, didn't you?" he asked from the kitchen.

"Whipped cream?" About a million possibilities blasted her mind at once, none of them innocent.

Chapter Four

ॐ

In excruciating pain, thanks to a pair of tight balls, Jeremy took refuge in the kitchen. He knew she would follow him, and he also knew it would take a while for the effects of Hope on his more sensitive parts to ease, so he called out, "You stay put right where you are. I want to surprise you."

Hoping he'd find a way to her heart through her stomach, and banking on the fact that every female he'd ever known, his mother included, had a weakness for chocolate, he hurriedly found the ingredients he'd included on her shopping list. He answered her occasional question about his activities with vague reassurances that she'd enjoy the results, and worked fast. Finally, with a quick shot of whipped cream from the pressurized can, he topped off the dessert, found a spoon in the drawer and hid both glass filled with chocolate and spoon behind his back as he headed toward the living room.

Thankfully, his painful erection had reduced, somewhat. His balls were still tight but weren't so bad he feared they'd implode on the spot like they had been earlier.

Hope Hart was one dangerous woman, even if she didn't know it yet. His heart warmed at the memory of her sweet confession. It had been so much more difficult than he'd expected, getting her to agree to sharing her fantasies. He wasn't sure what experience had stolen away some of her confidence with men, but he was determined to help her rediscover it, no matter what it took.

His Hope Hart shouldn't ever drop her gaze, at least not from him. He wanted her to feel confident enough to meet his gaze eye to eye, always.

He'd push her just a little each time, slowly ease her from her shell. It might be frustrating, and he would probably suffer several more cases of blue balls before it was all said and done, but what else was he to do?

He couldn't allow her to hide her insecurities — whatever they might be — behind sarcasm any longer.

With his course set in his mind, he walked into the living room. Hope was sitting on the couch, watching television. She swiveled her head to look at him within a second of his entering the room. He could read her expression, at least he figured he could. She looked wary and nervous. That was not the reaction he was hoping for. Not after having given her that back rub and reassuring her as best he could that she had no real reason to be fearful.

Clearly it would take more than some carefully selected words to gain her confidence.

He drew the wineglass full of chocolate bribery from behind his back. Maybe this would help.

Her face lit up at the sight. All traces of uncertainty vanished completely.

Score!

"Oh, that looks wonderful," she said.

"It's my infamous mud pie. I had to use instant pudding, so I hope it's okay." He handed her the stemmed glass and spoon.

"I'm sure it'll be fine. Thanks." She dug right in.

He watched as she lifted a spoonful of chocolate and whipped cream to her lips and licked them with anticipation. He mirrored her, licking his own, and wishing he could get a single taste of her. Only one taste to take back with him to the other side.

It was so different there, so dull and empty. Sounds and sights and smells were flat compared to this side. And the joy of being touched...he'd forgotten how it felt to touch and be touched. It had been so long. Nearly six years now. His fingertips still burned after having finally felt warm flesh again.

For a brief instant he'd thought he'd gone to heaven as his fingers had traced the silky skin of her jaw, and tangled in the curls at her nape.

He shoved aside his thoughts for the moment and concentrated on watching Hope eat the dessert he'd made. Exactly as he'd hoped, she appeared to be enjoying every mouthful. Her eyelids were closed, leaving her long sooty eyelashes fanning over her milky white cheeks tinted a light pink. Her lips were slightly pursed, as though she might be waiting for a kiss. He briefly considered tilting his mouth over hers but shook away the idea. It was too soon.

For now, he would be content with the pleasures of watching her and stealing the occasional innocent touch. That alone was both ecstasy and agony. He couldn't imagine what making love would feel like with his almost painfully acute senses.

Her flavor would fill his mouth, her scent his nose. Her touches would set his skin aflame.

The corners of her mouth lifted into a soft smile and he swallowed a sigh.

"This is absolutely sinful," she murmured. "What a reward." She blinked open her eyes and met his gaze.

Happy to have her looking him in the eye again, he smiled. "I'm glad you're enjoying it."

"Very much. The whole dinner was wonderful. I've never tasted such delicious food. You're amazing."

"Thanks. But you haven't had my best yet," he joked, winking.

"If you're talking about food, I can't wait."

By the time she'd polished off the dessert, she looked satisfied but uneasy again. He could guess why and not wanting to make her suffer, he said, "It's time to turn off the CD."

Her eyebrows shot high on her forehead. "It is?"

"Yes. But first, let me have the name of your next customer so I can do my private eye thing on the other side. Having more than a handful of hours for the next one would be nice, even if the spirits you've been trying to call tend to hang around here."

"Sure...okay." She stood, set the empty glass on the coffee table and walked to her computer.

He stood next to her desk, listening to the clickety-clack of her keyboard as she looked up the information she had on her next customer.

"This one's a toughie. I received a call from a woman who's been looking for a child she had given birth to when she was a teenager. The child was put up for adoption but she understands that she died young from an inherited condition the mother had known she carried. The mother wants to tell her daughter she's very sorry for having put her through so much suffering. She's told me all this. It's a very heartbreaking story."

"Yes. I imagine it is. The mother's name?"

"Mary Anne Johnson."

"Johnson? That's a very common name. This isn't going to be easy. The child?"

"April."

"Okay. I'll see what I can do. Go ahead. I'm ready. Switch me off. I'll see you tomorrow at exactly seven again."

Hope nodded but didn't reach for the player yet. "Thank you for a wonderful evening."

His heart swelled. "You're welcome."

"I thought you were going to ask… I mean…I thought you wanted…"

"I do. But I'm willing to wait until you're ready. Assuming I don't die from the worst case of blue balls on the planet first," he teased as he stepped closer and took her hands in his. His gaze focused on her wide emerald eyes, he kissed each fingertip. "You have no idea how much I want you, Hope."

Silent, she nodded.

Then he released her hands and pointed at the player. "Think about the next fantasy you want to share with me, tonight as you lie in bed. Will you do that for me?"

"Yes."

"Goodnight, love. I'll see you tomorrow."

He wrote up a short shopping list for tomorrow's dinner then waited anxiously for the agony of changing back. It started a split second after the sound cut off from the speakers. A sharp prick in his head, then more and more until it felt like every atom in his body was exploding. Electricity buzzed and zapped up and down his quickly fading spine. Heat fanned out to his fingers and toes as he was literally pulled apart, cell by cell. The agony may have only lasted a few seconds, but as was always the case when a human suffered extreme pain, it seemed like each millisecond lasted a hundred years.

And then he was on the other side. Physically, his pain was over, but emotionally it was not. Now, with Hope so close yet unreachable, the pain of being apart from her burned his heart. The intensity of the pain shocked him. Could it be he'd felt more than lust for her all these years?

The answer came to him on a whisper, from somewhere deep inside himself. *Yes.*

On this side, every sensation was dulled. Colors showed themselves in varied shades of gray, sounds were muffled, scents so muted they were almost obliterated, and touch... completely gone.

He watched her as she stared with wide, unseeing eyes...right at him, yet he knew she could no more see him than she could the dozen or so other spirits milling about him. His fingertips itched to feel the satin warmth of her cheek. His nose burned with the need to catch her sweet scent. His arms ached with the need to embrace her.

Finally, she turned away, returning to the isolated existence only he knew her life to be. She hid her loneliness so well, even from that girlfriend of hers...and herself. Despite the latent psychic gift she wasn't aware she possessed, quitting a job where she enjoyed occasional human contact hadn't been a great idea. Now she spent most of her days in sloppy sweats, her hair gathered on the top of her head in a ponytail. She rarely ventured out of the house. It wasn't normal. It wasn't healthy. She didn't see it, but he knew her life force was slowly fading.

Like she did most nights, she flopped in front of the television and watched some old movie until she finally fell asleep. He watched her as she dozed, reached for her and stroked a numb, transparent finger along her jaw. She didn't stir.

He bent low and whispered in her ear, "Sleep well, sweet one. I adore you."

She didn't stir. She showed no signs of hearing him, still he continued.

"Why have you closed yourself off from the world, Hope? From your friends? Family? What happened?"

He could see her even breaths in the slow and steady rise and fall of her chest but couldn't hear them. Naturally, she didn't answer his question. He hadn't expected her to. But someday he hoped to have the answer, to understand what she was protecting herself from.

"I want more than this miserable life for you, Hope. You deserve so much more than what you've given yourself here." But would she take what he was offering? As he looked down at her, his heart clenched. She had to. The possibility of an eternity without her stretched out in front of him. No. That was *not* an option.

He snuggled the blanket up around her chin and then turned to find the child, April.

"Anyone here named April?" he called out into the muffled quiet. A dozen heads shook their answer.

One, a young girl with long hair and large, round eyes nodded. "That's me. I saw you on the other side. I have a message I'd like you to deliver."

* * * * *

Hope found herself looking forward to seven o'clock more today than yesterday, and not because of the woman on the other end of the phone line. While she was anxious to see what Jeremy found out, if anything, about her daughter, she was more anxious just to see him, to talk to him, to enjoy his company.

Last night after he'd gone, she realized for the first time how quiet her house was. So silent. So empty. Despite his claim that there were bunches of spirits milling about her all the time, she had felt alone. She'd never felt that way before. She'd even put in an emergency nine-one-one-I-need-to-talk-right-now call to her best friend, who didn't answer her phone.

"Maybe I need to get myself a couple dozen cats and name them all Sparky."

"What was that?" the woman on the phone asked.

"Oh, sorry. I was just...trying to communicate with the spirits."

"I see," she responded flatly but patiently.

Hope double-clicked the clock in the corner of her computer screen. "Just another minute."

"I didn't know the spirits followed a schedule," Mrs. Johnson said with a curious tone.

"The one I communicate with does. He's sort of a courier, contacts the spirits I'm searching for and delivers messages back and forth."

"How interesting. You have your own ghost delivery man."

"Yes," she said, watching the seconds tick off. Ten more! Her heart skipped a couple of beats as she imagined him standing right beside her, waiting for her to turn on the CD. What did he see, hear, feel on the other side?

Five, four, three...

"Okay, I'm going to call him. You hang on for just a minute, Mrs. Johnson. I'm going to put you on hold. It may be a few minutes before I have something for you."

"I'll wait. Thank you."

She hit the "hold" button on the phone and then the "play" button on the CD player. Unlike the last couple of times, this time Jeremy was standing where she could see him as he materialized. For a brief instant she caught a pained look on his face. Did passing through from one side to the other really hurt? She'd thought his comment about the pain was only a tool used to manipulate her.

As he solidified, her heart leaped in her chest, thudding against her breastbone and ribs. A smile pulled at her cheeks. "Hi," she said.

He didn't speak right away, and she wondered if he was okay.

Her smile fading, worry a heavy lump in her belly, she slowly stood. "Are you okay?"

"Yes," he said, not looking okay at all. Yes, he was still as stunning as he had been last night, but she sensed something, a darkness, whether it was from pain, or sorrow, or whatever. "I'm fine. I found the child your customer was searching for."

"Good. But are you sure there's nothing wrong?"

"I'm fine." He gave her a reassuring, if not halfhearted smile then pointed at the blinking red light on the phone. "Do you have someone waiting?"

Still trying to read the fine lines etched into his forehead and around his eyes, lines that hadn't been there yesterday, she mumbled, "Yes…"

"Shouldn't you get back to your call? I can give you the message after you're through with your call."

"Oh! Yes." She looked at the phone, hoping the woman hadn't hung up, angry. She picked up the receiver and hit the button, taking the call off hold. "Hello? Mrs. Johnson, are you still there?"

"Yes."

She breathed a sharp sigh of relief. "I'm sorry I kept you waiting so long. I have heard from the messenger. He was able to locate your daughter. He has a message for you."

"He does?" she sounded excited.

"Yes." Hope smiled at Jeremy and mouthed, "Go ahead."

He looked solemn as he said, "Her daughter has been trying to reach her."

Hope echoed Jeremy's words in the phone for the woman.

Jeremy continued, "She wants her mother to know that her death was not her fault, that she is grateful for the life she was given and she hates to see her mother blame herself for her illness and death."

Again Hope repeated Jeremy's words into the phone. In response, she heard soft sniffles and short huffs of breath as the woman quietly cried.

"She cannot rest peacefully until her mother releases her," Jeremy said. "She wishes to leave this world, to join the light but she cannot."

Hope nodded with understanding then said, "Mrs. Johnson, your daughter has asked you to please release her. Your guilt and sorrow have shackled her to this world, made her a prisoner. She understands your feelings and doesn't want you to feel bad but instead wishes you to be joyful, to celebrate the life you gave her and the life she wishes to have now. She would like to join the light, to leave this world." She heard the woman crying and stopped speaking.

"I've made her a prisoner?" Mrs. Johnson whispered.

"I know you don't mean to do that," Hope answered. "It's just the way the spirit world works."

"I didn't...I don't..." The woman sighed. "Yes. I will let her go now. I didn't know my guilt would do that to her. I thought I owed her something, since I missed so much when she was alive."

"You gave her the greatest gift of all. You gave her life." Hope talked to the grieving woman for another twenty minutes or so, thankful for Jeremy's strength and steadfast but silent support. Finally, the woman thanked her for her help and hung up the phone.

Sort of bobbing up and down in a muddy puddle of mixed-up emotions, she turned to Jeremy, at last able to give him her undivided attention. "What is 'the light'? And why haven't you gone there?"

He no longer looked so upset though he didn't look his usual goofy self either. "Are you hungry?" he asked, brushing his hands over her shoulders as he walked past her toward the kitchen. He obviously wasn't about to answer her question.

She wondered why. She decided not to push it for now. "Starving. I didn't eat a thing all day, wanted to save my appetite for dinner tonight."

"It's not good for you to skip meals." He caught a curl that had somehow wiggled free from the scrunchy on the top of her head and smoothed it between his forefinger and thumb.

Tiny tingles zapped up her arms and down her legs. Warmth pooled deep in her belly and her heartbeat skittered, trying to find its former rhythm. In that instant, she knew she was falling for this man, this dead man. She was falling fast and falling hard.

That fact was not particularly reassuring. What kind of future could she possibly share with him? What kind of future did she want to share with him?

She gave herself a mental shake, hoping to jostle herself from the grip of mucky emotions that had gripped her today and gently tipped her head until her hair pulled free of his grasp. "I'll be fine. If I sit around here on the computer all day and eat, I'll be a cow."

"Not a chance. And even if you did, you'd be the most beautiful cow in the world, in my eyes."

"You, dead guy, are a charmer. You know exactly what to say to a girl."

"What can I say? I've been practicing in the mirror." He winked then walked into the kitchen and began gathering ingredients for their dinner.

She flopped onto the stool at the snack bar just as she had the night before and watched after he refused to allow her to help. Again, she was mesmerized by the quick efficiency he moved with in the kitchen. As he had last night, he wore a short-sleeved T-shirt that was just snug enough to highlight the curves of developed shoulder and chest muscles. The sleeves were just loose enough to slide back when he lifted his thick arms, revealing the bulge of biceps encased in deeply tanned skin.

His butt looked as cute as ever hugged in his cotton khaki trousers.

He hummed as he worked — she couldn't name the tune. And looked completely at ease in the kitchen, in such contrast to how she felt in there. If a food couldn't be prepared in a microwave, it was too complicated for her to prepare. Jeremy, on the other hand, seemed to enjoy making everything — even pasta sauce! — from scratch.

She was in complete awe. But before she could really work up some good fantasies about the man she was watching, the doorbell rang, interrupting her daydreams.

The nerve.

"I'll get it," she told him as she slid from the stool and headed over to the door. After a peek through the peephole, she opened it and five foot-nothing of terror on two feet barreled past her.

Mandy grabbed Hope's upper arms and gave them a squeeze. "Oh. My. God. I'm relieved to see you're all right. After that message you left last night, I couldn't stop worrying."

"For someone overcome with terror, it took you long enough to respond," Hope teased, lifting her finger to shush her friend. "Glad it wasn't life or death or I might've bit the big one by now."

"That's not funny. You know what a disaster my schedule is."

"You work part-time."

"And then there's getting by eyebrows waxed. I can't miss that appointment or I look like a Neanderthal woman. And my manicure…not to mention shopping," she joked, like always.

"Wow. With a killer schedule with that, I feel fortunate you made it here at all." Hope winked.

"So…" Mandy's head swiveled on top of her long, narrow, swanlike neck. "What's the big emergency? You said you needed to talk to me. You sounded bad, let me tell you."

"I sounded bad because I was wondering if I've gone completely nuts."

"You've been nuts. No big surprise there," her friend teased. When Hope slanted her a halfhearted warning glare, Mandy said, "Okay, okay. I'm just joking. What's wrong?"

"This might sound a little crazy but I think I can see dead people," Hope whispered.

"I told you that before. Why do you think I suggested you do the psychic medium shtick?"

"Because you're a dork, honestly." Now it was her turn to grab her friend's arms and give them a squeeze… and a shake too for good measure. "Didn't you hear me? Let me say it again. I. Can. See. Dead. People. Sheesh, I sound like that kid in that movie with Bruce Willis. Man, oh man, just tell me I'm not dead and am wandering around unawares, haunting my own home. Pinch me or something. I need to make sure I can feel pain. I don't think ghosts feel pain—"

"Gladly." Mandy gave Hope's arm a painful pinch with her long, fire-engine red, newly manicured fingernails.

Hope squealed. "Oooouch! Okay, okay. Ease up, you barracuda. I think you might've taken a chunk of skin with those claws."

"You told me to pinch you. I figured you'd need a pretty hard one to be sure."

"Thanks, I think." Hope said, checking her arm for missing skin. Thankfully, all she found was a red spot.

"At least you can be pretty sure you're alive."

"Yes. But it doesn't help me with the seeing dead people thing. I wonder if only I can see him?" She caught her friend's wrist and pulled her through the living room. "Take a look in my kitchen and tell me what you see."

"Ooookay. But will you let me walk on my own?" Mandy said, stumbling along behind her.

"Sorry." Hope released her friend's wrist and stepped aside, letting her lead. She watched her friend's face for a reaction.

"So far, I don't see anybody. Dead or alive." Mandy tilted her head and sniffed the air. "But I'll tell you this. Something smells tasty." She rounded the snack bar and walked into the kitchen proper. "Oh my God!"

Still in the living room, Hope sent out a silent whoop of relief. *She can see him! I'm not hallucinating!*

"I can't believe what I'm seeing. Are you cooking? What is this, beef?"

"Huh?" Hope dashed around the snack bar and walked into an empty kitchen, empty except for herself and Mandy. "Where'd he go?"

"Who go?" Mandy said, plucking a chunk of meat from the skillet.

"Jeremy…" Hope spun around on her toes.

"Oh, this is yummy. Jerry? Who?"

"No, Jeremy." Sure he wasn't in the kitchen any longer, Hope ran through the living room to check her CD player. The CD inside was still playing. Although she had the volume turned way down, she could see it spinning inside the player. "Strange…"

"Oh, hi there," Mandy said behind her. "Hope, why didn't you tell me you had company?"

"That's what I was trying…" Hope spun around, catching her best friend gawking at Jeremy, who was strolling down the hallway toward them. "There you are," she said.

"Sorry. Had to use the restroom." His gaze hip-hopped from woman to woman. "Is everything all right?"

"Fine. Just fine." Hope hurried to Jeremy's side while studying her girlfriend's face for any sigh of disgust. After all, maybe what she saw was very different from what other people did. Maybe he looked like a rotted skeleton with but a few strings of stinking flesh holding together his worm-eaten bones. "Jeremy, this is my friend Mandy Hogard. Mandy, this is Jeremy."

"Nice to meet you," Mandy said, looking much too sparkly eyed suddenly for Hope's piece of mind. Definitely no disgust there. No sirree.

"Would you like to join us for dinner?" Jeremy asked Mandy.

She beamed in response. "Sure. Did you cook? It looks delicious. I hoped you don't mind but I took a little taste. Incredible." She plopped her little butt on a barstool and spun around to face the kitchen as he went back to work. "I've always been impressed by a man who knows his way around a kitchen."

"Laying it on a little thick with the dead guy, aren't you?" Hope whispered in her ear.

"Who's dead? Him? Jerald?" Mandy asked much too loudly.

"His name is Jeremy."

"Jerry, Jeremy, whatever, he's cute." Mandy gave him a grin. "You're lucky he wasn't an ugly dead guy with bad hair and rotting teeth. How'd you get him? Can I have one too?"

"No, he's not a pet, for God's sake."

"Thankless bitch. After everything I've done for you," her friend said, plastering on a fake pout that wouldn't convince Hope to loan her a nickel let alone drum up another sexy dead guy. "I want a sexy zombie too. This isn't fair." She crossed her skinny little arms over her chest and turned up the pout a notch.

"I can't give you one. It's not like I put in an order at a drive-through window and there he was."

"Bummer. But if you could figure out a way to do just that, you'd make a fortune."

"Besides, he's not a zombie. He's a...er, a solidified spirit, or something like that."

"Whatever he is, he's solidified for sure. So, what's he do all day here with you? Cook?" She snickered.

"Yeah...kinda."

Mandy's eyebrows nearly leapt off her forehead. Her voice rose to falsetto as she repeated, "Kinda?"

"We have a sort of arrangement. He's helping me with my work during the day and then he comes here at night."

"And?" Mandy asked, obviously staring at his butt as he bent down to take some rolls out of the oven.

"And cooks for me."

Mandy leaned closer and slid her a doubting glance. "And?"

"And nothing."

"No way. You have a guy who looks like that here every night and all you do is eat?"

"Well…"

"You can't lie to me. I've known you since you were playing with Barbies. Have you fucked him yet?" she asked much too loudly.

"No, I haven't," Hope said, her cheeks flaring.

Jeremy turned around and smiled at her, which only made them get hotter. "Not yet. But I'm working on her. You ladies realize I'm right here, can hear your every word."

"Yeah," Hope said, giving her friend a jab with her elbow. "He can hear your every word."

"Well, he doesn't seem to be embarrassed by my questions, are you, Jeff?"

"Who's Jeff?" Hope asked, shaking her head. "That's Jeremy. Jerrrrr…ahhhh…meeeeee. Got it? Shoot, you're terrible with names. You really need to do something about that. Someday it's going to get you into trouble. It's a wonder you even get mine right."

"Of course I'd get yours right. Who the heck could forget Hope Love Hart, for God's sake? Your parents should be shot."

Jeremy carried two plates full of food to the table and then added a third. "Dinner's done. Come and get it."

When they sat down to eat, Jeremy said to Mandy, "I heard you say you've known Hope a long time. Did you go to Canton High too?"

"No, my folks sent me to private school. Unfortunately."

"Don't let her fool you. She loved it," Hope added, noting her friend's exaggeratedly glum expression.

"Ha! It was harder than college."

"Which is why she gets to make more money working three days a week than I do working morning, noon and night," Hope explained.

For that, she received a guilty smile from Mandy. "Yeah, well. It's not like I haven't offered to help my dear friend, here. Hope's got a lot of pride when it comes to accepting favors from friends."

"I've noticed," Jeremy said with a nod.

"Okay, that's enough about me." Hope shifted nervously in her chair.

They all ate for a few minutes in blessed silence, for which Hope was grateful.

But all too soon, Mandy piped in with a question to Jeremy, "So you're a zombie, eh?"

"No, he's not a zombie," Hope said, before Jeremy could respond to that ridiculous question. "Would you behave yourself?"

"I wouldn't call myself a zombie, though it's an interesting comparison." Jeremy leaned back in his chair and crossed those yummy arms over his scrumptious chest, making Hope wish her friend hadn't shown up tonight. "As I tried to explain to Hope, I'm a spirit. A spirit's atoms are spread out wider apart, much like the gaseous state of an element. Somehow, the CD she has in her player allows my atoms to move closer together, to give me the appearance of being solid again."

"How incredibly interesting." Mandy nodded before asking, "Does it hurt?"

"Hmm?" he asked, a mouth full of beef and vegetables.

"Becoming…er, solid. Does it hurt?"

He swallowed. "Nope. Not a bit."

"I was wondering the same thing," Hope admitted.

"Why?" he asked, his gaze wrestling with hers.

"I just thought I saw…you looked uncomfortable when you were materializing or whatever it's called," Hope admitted.

"Oh really? Well, when you flipped on the CD, I was just finishing up a workout and my glutes were killing me." He flexed his arms to illustrate, even though those were not the muscles he'd mentioned. She wished he'd flexed his glutes for her instead. That would've been a nice sight.

"Workout? You can lift weights in heaven or whatever it's called?" Mandy asked, filling her mouth with food.

"Sure. Sad comparison, but it's like being a prison inmate. There's not much for a dead guy to do but float around talking to people who can't hear him or shaking chains and making noise to spook the living. At least lifting weights keeps me from getting bored. It does nothing for my physique, since I'm a spirit now."

"How interesting," Hope said, wishing she could visualize what his world looked like. "What's heaven look like? Sorry for all the silly questions. I've never been able to ask a dead person these kinds of things before."

"No problem. I don't mind a bit." He flashed both her and Mandy a toothy grin. "Besides, I'd rather talk now because later your mouth might be too busy to talk."

"Oh really?" Mandy teased.

Hope blushed furiously. She didn't dare slant a glance Mandy's way, knowing what kind of look her friend would give her.

What he was suggesting? Would it be more chocolate keeping her mouth busy or something else? Another wave of heat rippled through her body.

"First, heaven isn't a place, it's a state. Like I talked about before. The place is here, on this planet. But when I'm on the other side, things look, smell, sound different, dull and flat. It's kind of like comparing an old black and white silent film watched on one of those console TVs with the latest action adventure with all the super-duper special effects and surround sound watched in a state of the art movie theater. The first time I crossed to this side, it took me a while to get used to all the sensations. They were so intense."

"So, do you miss this world?" Hope asked around a mouthful of food. A part of her felt sad for him, after hearing how dull and gray his world was. Now she could understand why he'd asked to spend his nights with her, and why he'd been like an octopus, all grabby, touchy. He'd been a victim of severe sensory deficiency. Just being free of that foggy nothingness would be worth it, even if he wasn't so crazy about her. However, the understanding she was slowly developing about him and his afterlife made his early exit last night even more puzzling that it had been before. And that was saying something.

"Some parts," he answered, giving her a knowing smile.

Chapter Five

❦

Hope felt herself leaning in closer but her friend beat her to the question, as she asked, "Like?"

Jeremy's gaze tangled with Hope's and she felt herself drawn closer, called by the pain and turmoil, maybe confusion, she found there.

"What is it, Jeremy?" she asked.

He dropped his eyelids and when they lifted, she felt as if he'd drawn a blind. Though she could still see his eyes clearly, somehow he'd blocked her from reading his emotions in their depths.

What are you hiding and why? That was one nifty trick. Handy, but frustrating being on the receiving end. She wondered how he'd done that. She'd like to learn how. Might come in handy someday.

"I miss this." He slid a hand across the tabletop and lifted it in front of hers. Not sure what he was trying to do, but feeling like he wanted her hand, she laid it in his. His fingers twined with hers and he smiled, looked at their hands then at her face. "I miss touching. When I'm on the other side, I feel nothing."

"Oh, that stinks," Mandy said as she gathered her plate and silverware and went into the kitchen with them. "I think it's time for me to go now."

"Thanks for coming to check on me," Hope called, unable to move, to stand or even pull her gaze from his face.

"Thanks for dinner. I'll call you tomorrow," Mandy shouted from somewhere in the living room.

"Okay."

"Bye, Jeremy. Good to meet you."

"Good to meet you too," he said, not pulling his gaze from Hope either. "You have no idea how empty a person's existence can be just from lacking the simplest of sensations," he continued as she watched his fingers curl and uncurl around the back of her hand. "When I was alive, I took the sense of touch for granted, most of the time unaware of textures, temperatures and so on unless they were extreme or painful." His gaze captured hers again. "How often are you aware of the weight of your clothes, or the texture of the carpet under your feet?"

She glanced down at her bare feet. "Never."

He lifted their hands until they were both upright then uncurled his fingers and slid his flattened hand up and down against hers. The innocent touch sent sparks of awareness through her body. "Did you feel the rasp of my calluses against your palms?"

"Not until you mentioned it."

"Or the chill of the tabletop," he said, tipping his head to her left hand, which was resting flat against the table's slick surface.

"No."

He lifted his fingers to her hair, tugging the cotton scrunchy from it. Curls fell around her face, resting on her shoulders and cascading down her back. He gathered a fistful and pulled slightly. The tingling tension on her scalp felt wonderful, erotic. The little sparks of awareness flared into blazes of molten pleasure as she let her eyelids drop, partly obscuring her view.

"Your hair is so incredibly silky, like the finest satin." He lifted it to his nose and visibly inhaled. "Mmm... coconut."

"It's my shampoo," she whispered. She captured a stray piece and lifted it to her nose as he gently stroked her jaw with his thumb. "But I showered hours and hours ago...I don't...smell the scent any longer." It was getting increasingly difficult to speak thanks to the heat building inside her body. And he hadn't touched any vital parts yet.

"It's still there. You've just become desensitized to it." He pressed her strawberry curls to his lips, and enraptured, she watched. He hadn't touched anything but her hand, face and hair, yet she was blazing hot. Waves of need crashed through her body with blinding force. She hungered to be closer, skin to skin, breast to wide, hard chest. She wished he would gather her into his arms, hold her tight.

She wanted to taste him.

As if he could read her thoughts, he tipped his head and slowly lowered it. Dizzy and giddy, every cell in her body humming with anticipation, she closed her eyes, held her breath and waited for the moment their mouths met.

In a single heartbeat she felt his warm mouth press against hers. A flurry of emotions and sensations pummeled her at once. In response, she sucked in a deep breath through her nose and threw her arms around his neck. His supple lips slid over hers and his damp tongue traced the seam of her mouth.

Her lips parted and his tongue delved inside, finding hers and slowly stroking it. She moaned into their joined mouths, the sound echoing in her head, as spikes of tense, blinding need shot up and down her spine. Her pussy throbbed with the urge to be filled. Her breathing quickened and her heartbeat hammered an unsteady beat against her breastbone.

And in that instant she knew she would sleep with him that night.

As his hands slid down over her shoulders then skimmed along her sides, she dropped her trembling hands to his chest. Her fingertips traced the rigid line of his muscles, down the center of the wide expanse to the narrower abdomen. Through his thick T-shirt she could feel the definition of his abdominal muscles. Her mouth drawing in his sweet flavor, her hands splayed over his stomach, she was in agony and ecstasy both.

She sensed his waning control in the ripple of his tight abdomen, the swift speed of his tongue as it plunged in and out of her mouth in the steady rhythm of lovemaking. Feeding on his hunger, her own grew until she could no longer deny it.

She broke the kiss and forced her eyes open. Breathless and trembling, she looked into his heavy-lidded eyes. "Please, Jeremy," she whispered.

He lifted his hand to her cheek, palming it gently. His gaze searched her face for something. She couldn't guess what. "Are you sure?"

"Yes." She captured his hand in hers and placed it on her breastbone, letting him feel her racing, thumping heartbeat. "I want you to make love to me."

"Okay." He licked his lips and her gaze locked on his agile pink tongue as it slipped between them, swiped along their length and then disappeared again. "First will you promise me something?"

"What?"

"Afterward, will you tell me what you fantasized about the last time you masturbated?"

Hope's cheeks flushed a sexy shade of pink as she nodded. "Okay."

Hot, his whole body tight with building need, he scooped her up into his arms and carried her to her bedroom, the weight of her so right in his arms. He set her gently on the bed and looked down, his gaze taking a slow, twisty path down her body and then back up to her face. "You are so beautiful. So...perfect." Eager to see what lay below her clothes, he helped her sit up then lifted her pullover top over her head, leaving her nude from the waist up with the exception of her lace bra.

His fingertip traced the line of the cup as it cut across the top of her right breast and, breathless, he watched as she sucked in a quick, shallow breath at his touch. Seeming too heavy to remain open, her eyelids fluttered and fell over her eyes.

As he leaned closer and left a trail of soft butterfly kisses over her chest, he inhaled, drawing in her unique scent. Coconut, soap and the unmistakable scent of Hope, the wonderful combination so sweet he had to inhale over and over. He couldn't get enough.

His hands trembled slightly when he reached around her back and unhooked her bra, and his gaze dropped to tangle with hers as she lifted her hands to his shoulders. Emotions flickered across their emerald depths, stirring something deep inside him, something he couldn't yet name but something that had been lying there, quietly waiting for the right moment to reveal itself. Her fingertips dug at the muscles capping his shoulders before trailing down his arms and he groaned. The skin of his upper arms tingled, sending waves of heat through his body.

He could see she held her breath as he slid first the right shoulder strap down then the left. Her bra dropped from her breasts, hanging from her arms at the elbows. He gently pulled her hands from his arms to remove it completely.

She sat before him, nude to her waist, her arms at her sides, hunger and need darkening her eyes and spiking his temperature even higher. He couldn't imagine wanting a woman more than he wanted Hope. He wanted to touch her, taste her, hear her every breath. His touches flitted over the silky skin of her upper body, leaving trails of goose bumps in their wake. Her sighs made every muscle in his body coil tighter with need.

Her back tightened under his exploring fingertips and she pushed her breasts out in a silent plea for his touch. How could any man resist such a temptation? He answered by circling a nipple with his tongue.

Sweet heaven. He flicked the hard nub until she squirmed underneath him.

Sweet agony.

She cried out and caught the back of his head in her hands, tugging gently as she curled her fingers into tight fists. "Oh God," she murmured, over and over as he pulled her nipple into his mouth and suckled. First it was gentle but then as her cries grew louder, and his hunger intensified from a slight sting to a deep burn, he devoured her flesh hungrily. "Oh God, oh God, oh God."

His cock throbbing, screaming for release from against its fabric prison, he stopped a moment and looked up at her, the taste of her still tingling on his tongue. If he wasn't already dead, he could die happy right now. He whispered, "You're so sweet, love. So sweet." And then he moved to her other breast, alternately sucking and nipping until she was no longer squirming but all-out writhing.

She groaned again and fell backward, reaching for his shoulders but missing as she landed with a plop on the mattress.

The sight of her flat on her back on the bed, her eyes blinking open, searching for him, her cheeks and chest tinged a deep red, nearly sent him over the edge. Afraid of even the slightest movement, the rub of his cotton shorts against his cock, might make him completely lose control, he stood at the foot of the bed, immobile and mute.

She pushed herself up on bent elbows. "Jeremy?"

"I'm here, love. I just wanted to look at you. I want to see all of you. Can you take off your pants?"

She nodded and unfastened the button and zipper before sliding her jeans down over her hips. With fingers that were hardly more nimble than numb stumps thanks to his nerves, he helped her pull her pants down and then tossed them aside while she worked on removing her panties. Her legs were long, smooth, shapely and feminine, exactly how he'd imagined them. With a fingertip he traced a path from her hip to her ankle then back up again. A soft gasp slipped between her parted lips, kicking his heart into overdrive.

Now fully nude, she lay flat on her back visibly trembling, shivering. His hunger-filled gaze meandered over her flesh. His balls were so tight he thought they might burst. His head so soupy, his every thought but one became stuck in the sludge. *I want her. Now.*

"Absolutely perfect," he muttered. He licked his dry lips. "I want to see your pussy. Open your legs for me." He heard the tight restraint in his voice, could see how his command fed her hunger.

She slowly bent her knees and slid her feet up toward her bottom. Then she moved them apart, opening her most private parts to him. The spark of passion in her eyes set a fiery inferno in his veins. The sight of her slick folds, wet with her need, made his knees soften. He caught himself by bracing a hand on either side of her hips before he crumpled to the floor.

His tongue darted out to wet his dry lips again. Then, his whole being aching for a taste of her, he bent over her and rested a hand on each of her knees, gently drawing them up and further apart.

So open. So exposed. So sweet.

His cock throbbed a quick, insistent beat as he watched her squirm and moan under his searching gaze. He watched the subtle movement as her stomach contracted and relaxed, alternately tipping her hips up and down.

He imagined driving his cock into those hot folds and sucked in a ragged breath. "I love the way you smell and I can't wait to taste you," he heard himself say.

Her thighs trembled and she gasped when he gently parted her labia with his fingers and took a slow, lazy swipe with his tongue. Again, he found himself on the verge of losing total control.

This wasn't enough, not nearly. More. He needed more and he sensed she did too. He needed his cock pounding in and out of her, needed his fingers drawing slow circles over her clit, needed to bury his face in the crook between her neck and shoulder.

"Jeremy," she half-growled, half-spoke.

"Patience, love," he growled back, tipping his head up to meet her gaze. "I want this to be good for both of us."

He bent over her again, letting his tongue slide up her slit, and explore the sweet flesh surrounding her clit. The skin of her thighs was like silk beneath his palms. Her flesh like the sweetest fruit on his tongue.

He felt her shudder, felt the rasp of goose bumps against his palms as they covered the lower half of her body as he drank from her, dipping his tongue into her passage to taste her deeply.

She reached down and gripped his hair in her fists. "Jeremy!"

He chuckled, even as waves of hot pleasure fanned over his chest and stomach. "Okay, love. Is this what you want?" He pressed a finger into her slit as his tongue danced over her clit.

"Oh, yes!" She tipped her head back and drew her knees further apart in an obvious invitation for more.

He filled her pussy with two fingers. His tongue flickered over her nub as her heavy breathing and the musky scent of her pleasure sent rhythmic bolts of white heat up his chest. He heard his own gasping breaths and racing heartbeat in his head, felt his body tightening in ready, a powerful orgasm coiling like a tight spring in his belly, as he brought her to the cusp of release.

"Take your release. I want to taste your sweet juices as they coat my fingers and lips. Come now."

As if her body had no power to do anything but obey him, he felt her shudder beneath him, gripped by her orgasm. She tossed her head back and forth as her pussy convulsed around his fingers.

"Oh yes!" He lapped up the warm wetness seeping from her pussy then kissed a wet path up her stomach and chest. Straining against his own need for release, he pressed his lips to hers, the taste of her mouth only stirring more need within his body.

He could wait no longer. He slowly crawled over her, on his knees, straddling her hips.

She watched in awe as he lifted his shirt up over his head, revealing the beautiful upper body she'd only touched but hadn't seen.

Wowzers, what a sight! She'd seen bodies like that on the Internet and in magazines, even on the beach. But never in her own house, in her own bedroom.

To think he'd probably never change, never age, always remain so…perfect.

In order to get rid of the pants, he had to sit. He flopped onto the mattress, setting it into a quick series of bounces, after unsnapping and unzipping his pants. He wasted no time sliding them off. In an obvious hurry to get on with things, his legs curled up and, hiding the bulge of his equipment still snugged in black cotton briefs, from her searching gaze, he lobbed his pants across the room. Then he hiked up his hips, slid off his briefs and quickly disposed of them as well. When he raised himself up on his knees, his very large, very erect cock caught and held her gaze.

Holy crap, that was the biggest penis she'd ever seen, outside of the porn film Mandy had rented for her once as a joke.

She swallowed a lump in her throat that had formed out of nowhere. Her pussy spasmed. Her heart hiccoughed a few irregular beats before settling into a quick, steady pace.

She couldn't tear her gaze away from his cock as he gently urged her legs apart with his palms then teased her slit with the purplish head.

Would it hurt to have such a huge cock inside her? Or just feel amazing? Every muscle in her body trembled with anticipation as she waited to find out.

His fingers found her clit and teased it with slow, steady circles and just the perfect amount of pressure. Just when she thought she couldn't take another second of teasing, he pushed that glorious rod into her passage. It filled her so completely, so wonderfully, she sighed.

His thrusts in and out started slowly, giving her delicate tissues time to accommodate his girth.

Then, when her juices were flowing and her pussy eagerly taking him, he sped up, driving into her with more force. His hands roamed over her face, chest and his mouth followed the same path. He bit her neck and shoulder as he pinched her nipple between his finger and thumb.

She tipped her hips until his coarse pubic hair rasped against her clit and ground her mound into him, both taking him deeper inside and increasing the friction against her clit.

He groaned in appreciation and claimed her mouth with a breath-stealing kiss. "Tell me when, baby. I can't wait any longer.

"When! When," she repeated.

Together, they stroked and thrust their way to a mutual orgasm that left them sweaty and breathless and quaking in each other's arms.

Jeremy rolled onto his side, his cock still deep inside her, and pulled her into a tight embrace. He kissed her neck and shoulder, her temple, her eye, her nose.

After the blazing heat had cooled to a pleasant warmth, Hope sighed and smiled.

Jeremy's eyelashes fluttered like butterfly wings as he blinked open his eyes. Little delicate things on such a hard, angular, manly face. "Are you ready?" he asked in a husky voice that made promises good enough to make a girl shudder.

"For what? Round two?"

He chuckled. "No. Although in a few minutes, I wouldn't mind going another round...or two."

Two? Yay! "Then what should I be ready for?" She tipped her head back so she could look at his face.

"You promised to tell me about your fantasy. Remember?"

"Oh," she said to his chest. "Yeah. I did promise I'd tell you that." Her cheeks warmed. "I don't suppose you'd let me renege?"

"Not a chance."

"Didn't think so." She sighed again, although this time it wasn't because she was contented...and tingly... and sweaty all over. Testing his willpower, hoping to distract him, she clenched her inner muscles around his softening penis.

"That's not going to work."

"Darn."

"There's nothing to be embarrassed about," he said as he stroked her hot cheek with his fingertips. He pulled his wilting erection from her body. She felt instantly empty. Empty in a bad way. "Everyone has fantasies," he explained.

"You too?" She smiled. Another — granted probably not as fun — opportunity for distraction.

"Of course."

"Then why don't you tell me what yours is?"

"Because I asked you first."

That earned him a soft nudge in the belly, which of course he overreacted to. His dramatic moans of pain made her laugh, breaking the tension.

"You're a goof," she stated. *I like goofs.*

Years ago she'd made up a list of the qualities of her perfect man. Goof, or rather a man who could make her laugh, had been at the top of the list.

"Okay," he said on an exaggerated sigh. "This is my best offer. I'll tell you one of mine if you tell me yours. But you must go first."

"Okay. I suppose that's fair," she conceded. At least she wasn't the only one giving up embarrassing stuff. She'd learned a long time ago, handing over prime blackmail material while not getting any in return was a recipe for disaster.

She nuzzled his chest as she tried to remember the last time she'd masturbated. It had been a long, long, long time ago.

Years.

Then the memory started trickling back to her, like it had been held back by a faucet that had been twisted open a tiny bit. The scene came to her one dribble at a time. She'd been at home...watching some movie on TV...an obscure channel on cable...and then she'd gone to bed... and...oh yeah.

"I'd watched a movie about a woman who'd been kidnapped while traveling to some strange country...or dimension. I can't remember exactly. She was imprisoned for breaking a law she didn't know existed but was then taken to a palace, chosen to become the wife of the king of the country or whatever it was."

"Yes?" He looked intrigued. "I don't think I've seen this movie."

"I don't remember the title. Anyway, in preparation for the wedding, a group of women bathed her and massaged her with scented oils. Then she was dressed in long, flowing gowns and brought to the king. He was very sexy and powerful and he took control of her in bed. It was very erotic. I masturbated that night while imagining I was the woman."

"Mmm...Would you like to play out your fantasies someday?" he asked, stroking her arm.

"I don't know. A part of me would like to but another part wonders if the reality would be lame compared to the fantasy, you know what I mean?"

"I do. But I want you to think about it and next time tell me if there's a fantasy you'd like to live out. I want to make all of your fantasies come true."

"That's sweet." Actually, in a way he had already. She blushed again and avoiding his gaze, stared at his incredibly tight chest. His nipples like little pink arrows were just begging for a nibble. A nibble and a suckle. And his stomach too. The line etched down the center sure could use a tongue…

"…and that's my fantasy. Now, about tomorrow, what do you have for me?" he chattered.

"Huh?" she asked. She'd been so wrapped up in thoughts of his nipples and stomach she knew for a fact she'd lost track of the conversation. Who could concentrate on anything when such beauty was before one's eyes? Look at that navel. Had there ever been a more perfect belly button on a man before?

"What case do you want me to solve? What spirit do you need me to track down?"

"Oh! That!" she said, shoving aside thoughts of nipples and sexy belly buttons for a few seconds. "This one's a biggie." She wriggled out of his embrace and dashed on tiptoes into the living room, scooping up the newspaper she'd left sitting on her desk and bringing it back to the bedroom. She flopped onto her stomach and unfolded it. "See this article?" she asked, pointing to a huge headline on the front page. "I want to solve this mystery. This little boy is missing, disappeared a couple of nights ago. Supposedly kidnapped from his bedroom."

Jeremy rolled onto his stomach and she watched as he skimmed the article. "What makes you think he's dead?" he asked after he finished. "The police seem to think he's still alive."

"Gut instinct?"

"Gut instinct," he repeated.

"Yeah. It's just a feeling. I can't explain it. Did you read the facts? The stepfather was at home with the little boy when he disappeared—alone. The mom is a nurse, works the midnight shift. The stepdad said he was watching a movie on TV, didn't hear a thing. To me that sounds fishy. The neighbors described this little guy as loud and boisterous. Why wouldn't he make some noise?"

"Maybe he couldn't?"

"I don't believe that. The stepfather's involved somehow."

"But what about the fact that he's helping with the investigation, seems to be doing everything in his power to help them find the culprit?"

"Maybe he's giving them false leads? Trying to lead the police astray? You know, many cases of child disappearances are the result of family members or close friends abducting or killing them. The first guy I'd look at would be the stepfather." She pointed at the picture of her prime suspect in the newspaper.

When one of his eyebrows lifted as he slanted her one of those I-don't-know-I-think-you're-wrong looks, she added, "Something doesn't add up and I want to help if I can. Without your help, I wouldn't stand a chance of getting anywhere with a case like this. But you've given me an opportunity here, a chance to do something good. Look at this kid's mother." She pointed at the grainy photograph of a young woman. Even with the cruddy, blurry quality of the picture she could see what a mess the woman was. "This poor woman could spend years wondering what happened to her baby. And she has two other kids. What if the killer was someone she knows? Someone she trusts? Like her husband?"

He nodded. "I'll see what I can find out. But even if I can find the child, he may not remember what happened. Or if he does, he may not be able to talk about it."

"Okay."

"I'll try."

"That's all I can ask." She hesitated a moment then asked, "Is it hard?"

He shook his head. "Not yet, but if you come over here and give it a squeeze or two it might get hard again."

At first lost, she looked at his face. "Huh?"

He motioned for her to look lower, which she did of course, and caught a glimpse of one index finger pointing at his cock.

She laughed, rolled onto her side and took it in her hand.

Just as he'd suggested, a squeeze or two was all it took.

Chapter Six

ର

Hope woke up the next morning noticing one thing, the silence. It wasn't the kind of silence one would cherish, like the peaceful stillness after being in a room full of kindergartners for a full day. It was the kind of silence that reminded one of exactly how alone they were.

She briefly considered calling Mandy at work but knew at this hour she'd likely only get the lukewarm response of her answering machine's greeting. Not hardly worth the effort.

So instead, she tried to mentally embrace her aloneness, walked around the house nude—you can't do that with a houseful of people—and scratched any part she was so inclined to scratch. She even belched after she guzzled a great big glass of grape juice. This new sensitivity to being alone was making her worry. She liked being alone, needed to be alone, she reminded herself. Living with another person sucked. Depending on someone else, especially a man, for anything—money, happiness, love—was a surefire way to disaster. A one-way street to Heartbreak Hotel. She'd seen it happen too many times, in her own life, in her mother's, in Mandy's.

Shaking away the mental lead weights pulling down her mood, she headed for the bathroom. She had all the hot water she could wish for in the shower. Took extra long just standing there, enjoying the way the heat soaked through her skin and warmed her insides. And afterward, rather than get dressed and head straight for the computer like she normally did, she lay in bed nude, catching the scent of Jeremy and sex still lingering on the sheets, and masturbated.

When she closed her eyes and let her imagination carry her away, she didn't travel to a faraway kingdom or the scene of some natural disaster crawling with hunky firemen. Instead, she was in a gray place where sounds were muffled and colors muted. And she was with her phantom lover, Jeremy.

As she brought herself to climax, she let him live out one of her most secret fantasies. He tied her up, her legs oh-so wide, and fucked her ass and pussy at the same time. Her ass with a dildo, her pussy with his sweet rod.

Her orgasm was powerful, more than satisfying, yet not as great as last night's. Still tingling, she dressed, combed her hair and went to her computer to start work.

When she clicked her email, she was surprised to find dozens of messages, new customers, each referred by the two she'd helped this week. And her voice mailbox was brimming with messages too.

She couldn't wait to tell Jeremy!

At six o'clock she rushed to her room, took a second shower, shaved herself smooth—everywhere—and put on a sexy dress with a neckline that plunged between her boobs to almost her belly button and a skirt that barely covered her butt by mere inches.

A pair of stilettos—at least she wouldn't be walking anywhere in them—some makeup and her hair dried, curled and teased a bit and she was ready for Jeremy.

He'd be here in just a few minutes!

This time, despite the fact that she found him absolutely irresistible in the kitchen, especially when he wore her mother's old ruffly apron, she ordered a couple of slabs of ribs from her favorite delivery joint.

With seconds to spare, she positioned herself in her chair, her legs crossed to show off most of her thighs, one arm slung over the back of her chair in typical Hollywood starlet fashion, and rested her finger on the play button of her CD player. She slanted an eye at the clock on her computer screen and waited.

Oh boy, she was a bundle of nerves. She couldn't remember ever being so excited to see a man. Her insides were doing flip-flops like a room full of gymnasts. Her hands were shaky and cold, her palms slick with sweat. Her heartbeat thumped in her ears.

At exactly seven o'clock she pushed the button. The first to appear were Jeremy's feet, then shins, knees, thighs, and up. The last part to appear was his head. Again, she caught a brief instant of agony on his face as he became solid.

But as quickly as the expression appeared it disappeared, replaced with the kind of smile that sent her heart to her toes and then rebounding all the way up into her throat.

"Hi," he said.

"Hi," she answered.

Awkward silence dropped like a hunk of lead between them. She tugged at her short skirt.

His gaze dropped to her lap, clearly drawn there by her movement. He licked his lips. One side of his mouth quivered slightly as his gaze shifted to her face. "You look...wow...incredible. You shouldn't have gone to the trouble."

"Thank you. But don't think for a minute I did all this for you," she teased.

"Oh yeah? Are you seeing another dead guy behind my back?" he asked in a joking voice as he lunged forward, caught her wrist and pulled her into a hug. He dropped his head and gave her shoulder a soft bite which made her yelp with surprise.

"What's wrong, a girl can't date other ghosts?" She jumped out of his arms and hooked a fist at his stomach, knowing he'd either dodge the blow or pretend to be fatally wounded. "And what's with the biting? You're no vampire."

He dodged the blow, caught her wrist in a grip as tight as a vise and yanked her back toward him again. "Sorry. I couldn't help myself. You look so delicious. Even if I'm not a vampire I'm tempted to take a little taste. How about letting me take a few more." He lowered his head for a second nibble but just before his mouth reached her neck, the doorbell chimed.

"Speaking of nibbling, that's our food." When he didn't release her, she shrugged her shoulders and wriggled away.

The doorbell rang a second time and she hurried toward the front door, checking to make sure her clothes covered all her vitals before opening it. No sense giving the delivery guy a free boob shot.

The young kid on the other side of the door gave her a friendly smile as he handed her the bag of food. She paid him with the cash she'd robbed from her emergency fund then shut the door.

Jeremy looked at the bag with glittering devil eyes. She liked the dangerous spark she saw in those eyes.

"What's that?" he asked as she stood and gaped for a few moments.

"Dinner," she answered when she finally found her misplaced tongue. "Since you didn't give me a shopping list yesterday, I figured that meant it was my turn to supply the grub. Sorry, but this is the best I can do. Unless you wanted burnt toast and soy milk for dinner.

"There's something to be said for soy." He wrapped a thick arm around her shoulder and tugged the bag of food out of her hands.

She leaned to the left a little, allowing his bulk to support her.

"I'll carry this." He inhaled. "Smells great."

"Hope you like barbeque ribs."

"No, I'm talking about you." He nuzzled her neck and she shivered as his hair produced a crop of goose bumps. Then he took a whiff of the bag. "Though the food smells pretty good too." He forced her to sit in her usual spot at the snack bar with a gentle shove then got busy dishing out the food.

"This isn't fair. I'm supposed to be doing that."

"What kind of slave would I be if I let you serve me?" he asked with a sly smile that suggested his last question could be taken in a completely different way, a naughty way.

She liked the way Jeremy's wicked mind worked.

Getting warmer by the second, she said, "I have some good news."

He looked up from his preparations and encouraged her to continue with an, "Oh yeah? What kind of news?"

"I have…" She shifted her gaze up to the ceiling. "Oh, maybe twenty new customers." Then she smiled at him and added an exuberant, "Thanks to you!"

"Twenty? Wow, that's great."

"Yep. All referrals from the two customers you helped me with this week. Not only will I make enough money to catch up on my bills, but I'll actually be able to get ahead a bit. I don't know how to thank you."

"Well, you just remember that gratitude when I tell you what I found out about that missing kid." He gathered their full plates and carried them to the table.

She followed him and sat down. "What did you find out? Was I right? Is he dead? Did he tell you who did it? It was the stepfather, wasn't it?"

He shook his head. "I tried. I couldn't find him."

"No way."

Nodding, he chewed and swallowed a mouthful of meat and roasted potatoes. "Either he's still alive somewhere or he's wandering lost, far away from home. I looked around here and around his home. Didn't find a trace of him."

"Well, shoot. So much for my idea about helping solve a big case." Puzzled, she thought about the details of the case she'd read in the newspaper as she ate.

Jeremy did his best to distract her, God love him. But she couldn't stop thinking about that sweet little boy. If Timmy Davison was alive, where was he?

After dinner, Jeremy suggested they try going for a walk. It wasn't more than thirty degrees outside, if even that, so she dashed back to her room to get into some warmer clothes. He looked nervous as he took his first step outside. He looked more confident as he took his third, fourth and so on.

As they strolled down the sidewalk, her hand warmly nestled in his, she continued thinking about the missing child.

"You didn't find a thing? Did you ask the other spirits around his home?" she prodded, hoping he'd recall some little detail, anything that would help her.

"Yes. None of them could tell me anything." His voice was clipped, short, like the way hers got when she wasn't telling the whole truth and didn't want to be asked to explain herself.

Ha. I've gotcha. What are you hiding from me? "You mean there were dead people hanging around his house night and day, around the clock, twenty-four-seven, yet they didn't see a single thing?"

Jeremy's answer was a shrug.

So that's it. Trying to hide a bruised ego because you couldn't get them to talk. "Ah, you got the brush-off."

"Did not."

"Did too. Someone had to have seen something. They're lying if they told you they didn't. But why would ghosts lie to you, another ghost? What would they think you're going to do with the information? Turn them in to the bad guy? It's the slum mentality in spirit world."

"I guess."

"They're dead, for heaven's sake. It's not like the bad guy's going to kill them again. What're they afraid of? Chickenshits. Won't help a girl who's just trying to find a kid killer—"

"Okay, okay. They didn't lie. I'm lying."

She stopped walking and jerked her hand free of his grasp. "What? You lied to me? Why?"

"To protect you."

"Protect me? From whom? The kidnapper isn't after me. Why'd you lie?"

"I lied because you don't know what you're up against here."

"Then why don't you explain it to me? I'm a reasonable person. Give me a good reason to quit this investigation — if you want to call a little poking around in the spirit world an investigation — and I'll stop."

"Because..." He turned his head, avoiding her gaze.

Nobody, not even Jeremy, would get away with that. This was a prime example of why she couldn't trust anyone but herself. He'd lied right to her face. She stomped around him and stood on her tiptoes until her face was in his direct line of sight. "Because?"

He finally met her gaze. "Because I know if you heard the truth it'd make you want to go find that kid even more. And then you'd be in real danger."

"Oh come on." She tossed a dismissive hand in the air. "Real danger? I'm not going to go all Rambo and take on the bad guy myself. I'll just feed the information to the authorities. How much danger could I be in by doing that?"

"More than you know."

"Would you quit talking in circles?" Suddenly anxious to get home, she doubled back and headed in the direction from which they'd come. "If I didn't know better I'd swear you were trying to hold me back. I tell you I'm enjoying a little success and you start pulling back, holding things from me."

It took him two long, loping paces to catch up to her. "This has nothing to do with your so-called success. Though I should warn you to beware of what you wish for."

Oh! She did not appreciate being talked to like she was a brainless twit. "Yeah, yeah. Heard it all before. You might just get what you're wishing for, and yadda, yadda, yadda. Thanks, but I don't remember bodyguard being among the functions in my definition of slave. No offense, but I don't need anyone protecting me. I've done just fine protecting myself all these years, thank you very much."

"True, but you haven't been nose to nose with the likes of Karl Bergmann."

"Who's Karl Bergmann?" Once again she found herself screeching to a halt, this time mid-stride, which nearly sent her tumbling into the mucky brown snow skirting either side of the sidewalk.

"The guy responsible for the child's disappearance. He was the neighbor, lived across street. You were wrong about the stepfather, by the way."

"Oh well. You can't win them all. At least you finally gave me a name. Thank you." She started walking again, this time really speeding up the pace. She had to write down that name before she forgot it. She was terrible at that, much like Mandy. It was like names just bounced off her brain like rubber rather than sinking in. "I'll take his name to the police and let them take it from there. See? There's no reason to get all testosterone and overprotective on me. I know I'm no Nancy Drew. I won't play amateur detective and go chasing after the bad guy all by myself."

"But you see giving the police that name'll get them nowhere."

"Why?"

"Because he's not alive."

If she had rubber on her shoes, she would've heard the screech, like locked up tires on wet cement, when she stopped walking for the third time in the past ten minutes. "A dead guy did it? How?"

"I'm guessing he wasn't dead at the time."

"So where does that leave the kid?"

"I don't know. I didn't ask."

"Why not?"

"Because Bergmann's dangerous. I don't need him realizing what I'm doing and following me, finding the way back into this world. Could you just imagine what kind of havoc a guy like that could cause?"

"No. Why don't you tell me."

"He can't be killed by a bullet."

"But I can just shut off the player and he'll fade away, just like you."

"I'm walking out here now. I didn't fade away. Your player is almost two blocks away from here."

"I didn't even think of that. How are you staying solid?"

"I'm not sure. But my point is, if I can materialize and walk free around this world, so can he. He may even be stronger, if what I've heard about evil spirits is true. And your normal means of killing someone won't work on him. So he'd be free to run amuck in the world, committing God knows what horrible crimes."

"What are the chances he'll find me, though. Really? He's probably far away, wherever he hid the little boy."

"Could be. Just don't speak his name again. Hell, don't even think it. I don't want to risk you calling him here. I didn't mention this but I probably should. All the other spirits you were looking for—every single one of them—were in your house. I didn't have to go far to find them."

"I brought them here?"

"You did. Like I said, you have a natural gift. Even if you can't hear spirits, you're able to beckon them. Problem is if you call the wrong spirit, your gift becomes a curse. And not just a curse to you."

Chapter Seven

ഇ

Hope slumped into the billowy softness of her couch and tried to sort out the information she'd just been rather brusquely dished by a lying, overprotective dead guy.

She wanted to stay angry with him for not telling her the whole truth at first, but she couldn't. For one thing, he'd come clean so quickly. His brief foray with deception hardly rated him a lowdown, lying fink.

Besides, he was too darn sweet. Even now, he was watching her with worried lines etched deep in his forehead.

Time to end his suffering.

"Thanks for trying to protect me," she said.

His face lit up with visible relief. "Then you understand why I was hesitant to tell you?"

"I understand I'm dealing with powers I'm not familiar with. And I understand your wanting to protect me. But I want you to understand that lying to me—about anything—is never a good idea."

"I know that now."

"Good."

"Then all's forgiven?"

She saw her opportunity to milk him for a little extra TLC, and being a woman, she wasn't about to let that opportunity pass. "Almost. I think you owe me a favor or two if we're going to call things even."

"Oh yeah?" The lines of worry faded and an altogether different type of expression spread over his face. One of wicked pleasures. She liked that expression much better. "And I have a favor or two in mind."

"Is that right?"

"Yep." His long legs carried him across the room in a few strides. And before she had time to react, he had her off the couch and thrown over his shoulder.

The man had a real thing about sweeping a woman off her feet...not that she minded. She giggled as she bounced on his shoulder down the hallway to her bedroom. And when a firm smack landed on her bottom, she yelped in surprise. It only stung a little but it surprised her a lot.

He lowered her to the bed then stood over her, two thick arms crossed over his hunky, luscious chest. "Get undressed, woman. I want to see you nude."

"Well, hello and how do you do, too," she said as she righted herself, straightening her top, which had sort of bunched up under her armpits. Her midriff was hanging out in the breeze.

"Don't you get it? I'm trying some role-playing. Don't tell me you're not game."

"Role-playing, eh? So, who are you supposed to be?"

"I'm the big scary slave master."

"Ooooh, and who am I?"

"Silly question, slave." He lunged forward, flipped her on her belly, wedged his knee between her legs, and gave her bottom another sound smack. "That is for your sarcasm, slave."

At least this time she saw it coming and was able to refrain from screeching out like a frightened toddler. When the big scary master released her, she giggled as she gathered her arms and legs closer to her body and rolled over onto her back. When her gaze was captured by his, the giggles stuck in her throat.

She coughed a couple of times to clear them away.

"You dare laugh at me?" he bellowed.

Wow, that was pretty convincing! His gravelly voice rumbled through her body, setting all the good parts aflame. She liked this game already. "Sorry?"

"Sorry?" He rested one knee on the mattress, then the other one. Finally, he dropped his upper body over her, holding it up with his arms. His broad chest was less than a foot from hers, even closer if she arched her back just so. "Sorry?" he repeated.

"Sorry for being sarcastic?"

He dropped closer until his nose was no more than a hairsbreadth from hers. "Sorry, who?"

"Oh! I get it now. Sorry, Master." She let a giggle loose but squelched a second one when he gave her a warning glare.

"No giggling, slave. You should be trembling in fear of my awesome power."

"Oh believe me, I'm trembling. But not from fear." She wrapped her legs around his waist but no sooner did she get her thrumming pussy pressed against his rigid bulk than he caught her ankles and gently set them back down until the soles of her feet were flat on the coverlet.

He frowned. "Come on! This is your fantasy. You could at least try to play along."

"I am. Say, I don't remember telling you I fantasized about being a sex slave." She propped herself up on her bent arms.

"You didn't. But I know I'm right about this. It's your fantasy all right. But it seems I'm not hitting the right buttons. You're not squirming."

"I would be if you just touched me."

"No, no. This isn't right. I'm not...Intimidating enough. Yeah. That's it." He stood up and paced the floor.

Not sure what to do, she propped herself on some pillows and watched him as he mumbled to himself. Finally he stopped pacing and grinned. "I have it! Assuming I can actually walk out of this house alone without fading to a shadow."

"Where are you going?"

"It's a surprise." He hurried from the room and she followed at his heels. When he reached the front door, he threw it open. But he hesitated before stepping through the doorway. "I've been outside with you but not without. I'm not sure what might happen." He gave her one final longing look then put one foot over the threshold.

She watched his foot, half expecting it to fade away. "Looks like you're good."

"I'll be back in a bit. Take a bath while I'm gone. I want you sweet-smelling and fresh when I return." He strode through the doorway and out into the deepening night.

Wondering where the heck he was going at this hour, she watched his retreating back, then shut the door. It was absolutely frigid out there, cold enough to chill her simmering blood.

Then the memory of him looming over her, that naughty spark in his eye, warmed her all over again.

"You better get your butt back here in a hurry, Master."

* * * * *

About an hour or so later, Hope was beckoned from the bath by a loud knock on her front door. Knowing she hadn't locked the front door, since she wanted to make sure poor Jeremy wouldn't be caught standing out in the freezing cold while she soaked in a hot tub, she immediately questioned who was at the door.

About ready to be a prune, she hopped out of the now lukewarm tub and wrapped herself in her fluffy pink terrycloth bathrobe. She twisted a towel around her sopping wet hair and hurried to the front door, which was now in danger of being shaken from its hinges by whoever was on the other side.

"Easy, easy! No sense causing permanent damage. I'm coming!" she said as she hurried to the door.

She gripped the latch for the deadbolt and peered through the peephole.

Was that the grim reaper on the other side of the door?

Whoever it was had his back turned toward the door. He was wearing a big black cape with a hood so she couldn't see his hair.

"Jeremy?" she called through the door.

He didn't speak. He didn't turn around.

No way she was opening that door now. She flipped the bolt, securing the door. "Jeremy, if that's you out there, you're not being funny." Determined not to play into whatever plan he had going, she stomped away from the door. As an afterthought, she ran through the kitchen to bolt the other door. But before she reached it, it flew open and in walked the cloaked figure.

Scared poopless, she shrieked, "Jeremy!" and jumped backward, pressing her spine against the refrigerator. She tried to make out his face but there was a dark mask covering it, not completely opaque but enough to obscure his features, even his eyes. Even though she couldn't see his face, she had no doubt it was him. Whether it was the way he moved, the way he held his hands, his scent. But the mask made him look sinister, inhuman, downright frightening. "You've made your point. Now quit with the scary monster stuff, will you?"

In response, he growled out, "You will do as I say, slave. Or you will be punished." From somewhere in his cloak he produced a cat-o'-nine-tails. The tails struck her kitchen counter with an impressive thwack.

She shuddered, from a strange mixture of unease and anticipation. Her lungs felt like they'd collapsed, wouldn't hold enough air, and she found herself gasping. The sound of her heavy breathing echoed in her ears. Yes, there was no doubt this was Jeremy. But he was sure acting different from the Jeremy she'd spent the last couple of nights with. What would he do next? Both nervous and turned on, she watched him for a hint of his next move.

"Did you hear me, slave?" He took one giant step toward her and she couldn't help pressing her spine harder into the rigid, cold surface of the fridge. The handle dug into her side so she shuffled a little to the left. He lifted a hand to her face and cupped her chin, tilting her face up. "So beautiful, my little plaything. What pleasures you will show me."

"You're really good at this playacting thing, Jeremy. Too good."

"Who says I'm acting?" he challenged. "Now, strip for me. I want to see your body."

She hesitated for a moment. One very short second. That was all it took. In a single, fluid motion, he swept his arms forward and pushed the loosely tied robe off her shoulders.

Erotic awareness shot through her body at the rough yet gentle handling, sending pleasant tingles to all the good parts of her body. Although she caught the front of the robe to her breasts before it fell away, her shoulders were bare. And even though she couldn't see his eyes, she felt the heat of his gaze on her skin.

"You will take that robe off at once," he demanded. "You must not hide yourself—any part—from me."

She felt her fingers loosening their grip on the fluffy material then felt the garment sliding south toward the floor.

Standing in her kitchen as naked as the day she was born before a cloaked and dangerous Jeremy made her pussy spasm. Wetness seeped from her folds, trickling down the insides of her thighs. She squeezed her legs together.

"You will now go to the bedroom and lie before me."

Deciding she really liked this game, she played along, "Yes, Master." She tried to hide her flabby butt from him by holding her hands over it as she walked.

He gave her back a tap with the flogger, not enough to cause real pain but enough to get her attention, and she stopped walking but didn't turn around.

"Didn't I just tell you not to hide any part of yourself from me?"

She dropped her hands to her sides.

"Better. Now continue. But walk slowly. I like to watch the way your hips sway as you walk."

Achingly aware of him watching her, she took each step slowly and deliberately, accentuating the natural sway of her hips. If he wanted to see a sway, well, by golly, he'd see the sway of a lifetime.

He grunted with satisfaction which sparked a second wave of tingles through her body.

When she reached the bedroom, she stopped at the foot of the bed.

To her surprise, he sat on the bed then motioned to her. "Bend over, slave. I will give you your punishment now."

The word punishment reverberated through her body like a shockwave. Her knees softened like butter left in the sun. "Punishment? But I did—"

"Do you dare to question me?"

She bent over his knees.

"That's better." He lifted the flogger and ran the leather straps through his long, tapered fingers. Mesmerized and breathless, she watched over her shoulder. Would he strike her? Would she enjoy it?

"Do you like being my servant, slave?"

"Yes, Master."

"Would you like to take my cock in your mouth, slave?"

She gasped at the thought of his giant cock in her mouth, at the sweet flavor of him filling her throat. "Oh yes."

"Very well. But you must endure your punishment first." He lifted the flogger.

She felt herself stiffen in anticipation. As he flipped his wrist, changing the direction of the leather straps through the air, she squinted her eyes and cringed.

The straps struck her delicate backside with a sharp but not excruciating sting, no more painful than a slap with an open hand.

A blaze of heat shot to her pussy and the inner walls clenched.

He struck her a second time and a third. With each impact, the heat in her pussy flared brighter until she her whole body burned with need.

Her legs trembled. Her arms shook. Her head swam. Cool wetness dripped down her inner thighs.

Jeremy set the flogger down on the mattress and parted her ass cheeks with his fingertips. "Did you enjoy your punishment?"

"Yes, Master."

"What?" he asked in a surprised voice, making her rethink her answer in a hurry.

"I mean, no, Master. Please don't hit me again. I promise I'll be a good slave and do as you wish."

"That pleases me. Now you may suck my cock."

Since she was so shaky, she needed a little help as she climbed off his knees and kneeled on the floor at his feet. He helped her get settled in position with gentle hands then stood up and removed his pants and underwear. He left his cloak on, merely parted it at the front opening to expose his long muscular legs and huge erect cock to her feasting eyes.

Her hands trembled as she lifted them to cradle his testicles. The coarse dark hair coating them tickled her palms as she gently weighed them. In preparation for taking the thick, purple-hued head of his cock in her mouth, she licked her lips.

"Take me into that sweet mouth of yours, love. Take your reward." He tightened his thigh muscles. She felt them flex under her fingertips as she skimmed them over the smooth skin.

She darted her tongue out for a shy taste. He tasted wonderful. She took a second, whirling her tongue round the flared edges of the head then drew a long, wet line down the blue line underneath, straight to the base nestled in a crop of dark curls.

He moaned in appreciation and gripped the base in his fist, pumping up and down slowly. She supplied the lubrication by wetting the head and shaft with her mouth. Up and down she slid her mouth, taking in his flavor and relishing it. She whirled her tongue round the head then delved the tip into the narrow slit, tasting salty pre-come. This time she was the one who moaned.

Watching him work his large hand up and down that glorious rod, his free hand gripping her hair and oh-so gently moving her head as his cock fucked her mouth, nearly sent her over the edge.

Her fingernails raked down the smooth skin of his thighs as his cock thrust in and out of her mouth. Her pussy spasmed, empty and burning to be filled. Air burst in and out of her lungs in short blasts. Her head floated in a fog of need.

Very suddenly he halted her motions and drew his cock away. She knew he was close to release, could feel it in the slick of sweat coating his skin.

She reached up and ran her flattened palms over his stomach but he pushed them away then stepped back out of her reach.

"Enough. Now you will lie down and show me your pleasure." He stepped aside to let her sit on the bed.

She laid back and bent her knees.

"Open them wider."

She drew her legs wider apart. Her pussy walls clenched and unclenched as warm dampness seeped out and ran down her perineum.

He caught her ankles in his fists and pulled until her ass was nearly hanging off the edge of the bed. Then he pushed her ankles apart and back, forcing her legs wider.

She was so open. She squirmed and clamped her eyelids shut.

"I adore your little pink hole," he said in a deep gravelly voice that made her shiver, hot and cold at the same time. "Would you like me to put this into your ass, slave? I'm feeling generous tonight."

She blinked open her eyes and glanced down. His fingers were curled around a narrow pink plastic vibrator. In reflex, her anus clamped tight. Her pussy thrummed with new urgency. "Oh…"

He produced a tube of lubricant, and setting down the vibrator, squeezed out a fair amount onto his fingers. As he smoothed the cool substance over her hole and surrounding tissues, she squirmed with delight. One of his fingers probed her folds, skirting her passage. She wanted to yell out in frustration.

"Lie still," he commanded.

She tried to quit her writhing, but her pussy was burning so bad she couldn't help tilting her hips up and down, up and down. She needed to be filled, stretched by a large, thick cock. "Please," she moaned. Her eyelids felt as heavy as lead. They fell closed.

Jeremy turned on the vibrator and held the tapered tip on her clit, nearly sending her into space. She cried out, her whole body tied into tight, trembling knots. But just before she found her release, he moved it away. "Not yet, love."

"You're killing me," she said through gritted teeth. Even her cheek muscles were tight. Trying to catch her breath, she lifted her arms over her head and fisted the coverlet.

"Easy, baby. I'll turn it off."

She heard the faint hum of the vibrator quit and breathed a shallow sigh of relief. But that relief was short-lived.

He pushed the tip into her anus, which she tightened instinctively against its stiff probing.

"Relax, baby. Take it in. Once I get it inside, I'm going to fuck you to heaven and back."

Between the effects of the raw hunger she heard in his voice and the slight, but pleasant burn as the vibrator slipped into her anus, she couldn't help shuddering. Her bottom felt wonderfully full, her pussy achingly empty.

And then he filled that void too, thrusting his cock deep and hard. In, out, in, out.

She arched her back and cried out as he quickened the pace until they were both there together, on the cusp of sweet release.

"Are you with me?" he asked between puffing, strained breaths.

"Yes, oh yes!"

"Now, baby."

The slight swelling she sensed at the point just before his release sent her soaring over the crest. Her muscles spasmed around him, around the hard vibrator, still buried deep in her hole. And those spasms continued for a wickedly long time. But eventually, they eased to pleasant twitches.

Jeremy removed the mask then pulled the vibrator from her anus and removed his cock from her pussy simultaneously and she suddenly felt very empty again. He set the vibrator on the nightstand then rolled toward her, gathered her to him, until the full length of her was snuggled warm and tight against him, and pressed a chaste kiss on her forehead.

She sneaked a shy taste of his sweat-slicked chest with her tongue. Salty, male. Yummy.

"Sleep, baby. Sleep," he whispered, running his hand up and down her back. "We have all the time in the world to discover each other."

"But the case. The little boy. We didn't talk about it."

"I'll do what I can."

"Promise?"

He hesitated for an instant, for more than a couple heartbeats, and then said, "Promise."

"Thank you." She knew she was smiling as she drifted off to sleep.

* * * * *

It took Herculean effort to force himself from her warmth. Every part of his soul screamed for him to stay there, with her, and never return to his world. But he could feel the ache in her heart for the missing boy as if it gripped his own. And despite his worries, he had made a promise. He never backed out of a promise. Never.

He would just have to be very careful. The safety of who knew how many people was at stake.

He gazed down upon her, stroked her silky hair, breathed in her scent, stole a quick taste, a swipe of his tongue on her shoulder, then turned and walked into the living room.

He shut off the CD, suffered through the change then went in search of information about the missing child.

As he worked, he couldn't shake the feeling he was being watched. It was him, Bergmann. He was there, waiting, somewhere close by.

Chapter Eight

ಐ

"Thanks for inviting me over. This is too cool. I'm geeked." Mandy shifted closer to the CD player and stared at it like it was made out of platinum or something. Wow, amazing."

"This is only a CD player, you goofball. Now turn around. You're looking the wrong direction. Usually he appears right next to me. He has to be close. The nearest spirit to me is the one to materialize so he has to make sure he's the closest."

"Interesting…" she said as she circled around Hope's back. Her forefinger tapped her chin. "Where is he coming from, do ya think?"

"He's here right now. Just not solid."

"How cool!" Mandy waved her hands through the air surrounding Hope. "Did I just slice him in two, I wonder? Puréed ghost."

"You'll have to ask him when he's solid." Hope glanced at the clock, giddy and tingly and anxious to see him again. Even though they'd been seeing each other regularly now for the past several weeks, each night as she hit the play button, her nerves tied themselves into knots and her belly did a little flip-flop. All day, every day, she looked forward to seeing him. She thought about him while she worked, while she bathed, while she shopped. They ate dinner, talked about her case, then made love until they were both exhausted and couldn't move a muscle.

She fell asleep in his arms every night.

"One minute left," she sang.

"I'm glad you changed your mind and let me come over. I would've been really, seriously mad at you if you'd kept this to yourself another day. You made me wait weeks as it is. Which isn't fair at all. Especially since this whole psychic medium thing was my idea in the first place."

"Yeah, well, we were just getting used to things. Now, we've got a routine. Just remember, you promised to make like the wind and blow as soon as the show's over."

"Yeah, yeah. Wouldn't want to cramp your love life." She rolled her eyes. "By the way, next time, do me a favor and spare me the sordid details, will you? I'll never be able to look at Jeffrey in the eye again."

"Jeremy."

"That's what I said. Or should I be calling him Master Jimmy now?"

"I don't think that's necessary," Hope said, ignoring the obvious error her friend had made yet again with his name. To heck with it. Jimmy, Jeremy. It didn't matter. Mandy wouldn't be seeing him again soon anyway, not if Hope had any say in the matter. She was merely satisfying her friend's curiosity this one time, let her watch him materialize. After tonight, Jeremy Burbank would be Hope's secret little indulgence, taking the place of her discarded habit of scarfing down a nightly scoop of Ben and Jerry's ice cream, and far more satisfying.

She checked the clock again. Twelve seconds. She settled her finger over the "play" button, ready. Eleven, ten…

"So, let me get this straight. He feeds you info from the spirit world, digs up the dirt for your customers and in return you fuck him."

"No! That's not how it is." Seven, six…

"Easy, you don't have to get all defensive. There's nothing wrong with that setup. I'd say you're the clear winner, no matter how you look at it."

Three, two… "We'll talk later. Watch." She punched the "play" button and spun around in her chair, watching for a sign of him near the floor. A pair of men's black shoes appeared beside her. "See here?" She pointed at them so Mandy could watch.

Shins covered in black denim came next, then thighs, groin, abdomen. The long black cape hung down his still translucent but quickly solidifying torso.

"Holy…I… Oh, shit," Mandy stammered.

Hope gave her a smug grin, stood and walked to her side, shaking your shoulders. "Didn't believe me, did you?"

"No. But I do now."

"Are you all right?" she asked, noting her friend's milky color.

"Yeah." Mandy nodded, staring at Jeremy as he slowly solidified. "Wow."

Following her friend's line of vision, Hope turned her head to watch him too, with just as much awe. She wondered if she'd ever get used to the amazing sight of him as he changed. It was awesome.

Shoulders seemed to form out of a fine gray mist that was slowly rising up from the floor. Then slowly his head formed. It was sometime then that Hope realized the man standing there in the room with them wasn't Jeremy.

Scared, she couldn't move for what felt like a hundred years. It was as if her thoughts, the impulses charging from her brain, were clogged, failing to reach her limbs. Then, when the man gave her a smug grin and sauntered across the room, she finally lunged forward to shut off the player.

He moved lightning-fast, swinging one thick arm at her. It hit her smack-dab in the belly and she toppled backward, landing on her rear end with a loud "oof!"

He laughed. It was a nasty, creepy cackle that made her shiver. "What's the hurry? I just got here."

"Mandy?" Hope said, hoping her friend would take advantage of her position, much closer to the player than she was at the moment, to turn off CD and send Mr. Scary back where he belonged.

"Yeah," she squeaked. "Hope, who's this guy?"

"I don't know. But I can tell you who I hope it isn't." She recalled the case Jeremy had never been able to help her solve, and the warning he'd given her the last time they'd discussed it.

Assuming her visibly scared shitless friend was not going to help her with the player, Hope scrambled to stand. "You wouldn't possibly be Karl Bergdorff...or was it Bergmann? Would you?" she asked in a voice that was much too small and shaky for her comfort. She sort of sashayed closer to the CD player, hoping he wouldn't notice where she was headed.

He noticed.

Again, he moved faster than her eye could follow — this guy obviously possessed some incredible reflexes — knocking her to her rear end long before she reached her destination. "You. Come here." He lunged at Mandy, wrapped an arm around her neck and pulled her snug against his front.

"Shit!" Hope's wide-eyed friend yelped. Her teeth visibly chattered as she stared at Hope. "You didn't plan this part, huh?"

"Noooo."

"Don't move," he growled at Hope when she started to stand. His hands gripped either side of Mandy's head. "It would take nothing to snap her neck."

"Fine. I won't move. Please, just leave. Let us be. You've got what you want, right?"

"Not quite." He hustled Mandy over to the player then said, "I need to make sure you can't send me back."

Hope met her friend's gaze and mentally screamed, *Shut it off!*

Her friend must've gotten her message, but the content was altered. Instead of just hitting the button, she threw her arms around willy-nilly, knocking the player off the desk. It landed on the floor with an impressive thud. The soft crackle of the CD stopped.

"Shit!" both Hope and the ghost said in unison.

"Did I do bad?" her friend yelled. Her hands rose to the man's arms. Her knuckles whitened as her fingers dug into still solid flesh.

"I'm not sure." Hope held her breath as she watched the man, eager to see him disappear.

He wasn't fading.

A satisfied smile spread over his mouth. He tossed Mandy aside, sending her reeling backward until she completely lost her balance and fell. Her head slammed into the wall and Hope cringed with sympathy.

She jumped up to get the CD from the player, but the man was one step ahead of her. Much closer, it was easy for him to hit the eject button and pull the item they both wanted from the slot.

Waving it like a prized trophy, he said, "Guess this wasn't as powerful as you thought." With a single, swift movement, he slammed his hand down toward the edge of her desktop.

She knew by the sound that he'd just shattered the plastic CD.

He tossed the pieces at her then strode out of the room, laughing. But before he walked out her front door, he turned sinister eyes on her and said, "By the way, you were right. Karl Bergmann. Nice to meet you."

He didn't shut the front door behind him.

The first thing Hope did was drop at her friend's side and ask, "Are you okay?"

Mandy winced and rubbed the back of her head. "Yeah. I think so. Who was that guy?"

"A creep."

"I kinda got that part. Was he supposed to come through the portal or whatever you call that thing?"

"No. And now that the CD is broken, I don't have a clue how to send him back. Or how to call Jeremy."

"Oh." Her friend looked at her with very sad eyes. "That's my fault, isn't it?"

"None of this is your fault. Jeremy tried to warn me but I wouldn't listen. It's my fault." Hope rested her spine against the wall and let her head fall to one side until it rested on her friend's shoulder. She felt the sting of tears burning the corners of her eyes.

Jeremy was lost to her! Gone! No more. And there was a psycho madman running loose, wreaking havoc.

"If only I'd listened to him instead of getting all greedy."

"You? Greedy?"

"Yeah. Greedy and stubborn. Bullheaded. I wanted to solve this big missing persons case so that I'd become a famous psychic, pad my bank account and pay my bills, have some security. I had this great plan. I used Jeremy, abused the power I'd gotten from that CD...then refused to listen to him when he tried to warn me. I didn't want to answer to anyone. I rebelled like a stupid teenager, did the exact opposite of what he'd told me to do. I kept thinking about Bergmann, said his name, called to him. I wanted to solve that case so bad. And I didn't want to admit that I needed Jeremy's help to do it. I wanted to do it myself. Now I've let everyone down, Jeremy, myself. That little boy. I deserve exactly what I got. Unfortunately, the innocent people of Canton are going to get more than they deserve."

"Well, if calling him was supposed to bring him here, it worked."

"Yes, but it wasn't supposed to go like this. He was supposed to come when I was ready for him. And the CD was supposed to be my weapon...the CD that is my only link to Jeremy. It wasn't supposed to happen this way. This wasn't the plan." Her friend gave her a hug, smoothed her hair then stood and gathered the broken pieces of plastic and handed them to Hope. "Do you think you could get another one?"

"I don't know. I bought it on eBay. I haven't seen one since."

"Let's check anyway." Mandy reached down and grasped Hope's hands in hers, giving them a sharp yank, pulling a reluctant Hope to her feet. They went to the desk and Hope flopped into her chair, both anxious to see if she could find another copy of the CD but also fearful of learning she wouldn't, which would make her loss of Jeremy final.

A part of her wanted to wait, wanted to cling to what little hope she had left.

Her fingers hovered over the keyboard but she didn't type in the URL.

"What're you waiting for? It's ebay dot com."

"I know the address, silly."

"Then what's wrong?"

"I'm scared."

"Scared of what?"

If only you knew.

"I've never seen you scared of anything. Heck, you just took on an unnatural evil force from beyond the grave!" She gave Hope a nudge. When Hope didn't type in the website's address, she said, "Okay. You. Out. Let me look."

Hope stood and set about a nice, brisk pace, back and forth behind her chair as her best friend called up eBay.

"Okay. What the heck was that thing called?" Mandy asked.

"Um." Hope halted her pacing for a moment to try to recall the exact title. "It was called Spirit...Callings. Yeah. That was it. I found it in the music category."

"Got it." She typed fast. The keys sung out, clickety-clack. Then she moved the mouse.

Hope resumed her pacing. "Anything?"

"Not yet. Give me a minute."

Hope walked to and fro a few more times. "Anything?"

"No. Do you remember what the seller's name was?"

"I saved it somewhere." Hope traded places with Mandy and opened the file she'd saved with the purchase information. "Here. sbjspirit." She skimmed the music auctions. "I can't find him. Darn it! I could've probably burned a copy. Why didn't I think to do that?" She looked to her friend for an answer, but received only a shrug and a couple of raised eyebrows.

"Is there any way for him to warp here without that CD?" Mandy asked.

"I wish." Suddenly exhausted, she slumped her shoulders and dropped her head in her hands. "I can't believe this happened. Can I rewind time and try it all over?" Again, tears stung her eyes. This time she wasn't able to dam them back. They flowed freely.

"Aw, sweetie. I'm so sorry." Mandy drew Hope into a hug, but it didn't comfort her.

Nothing would. Jeremy was gone, never to return. And thanks to her insecurities, a monster was running amuck, probably kidnapping children and doing God knew what with them.

Chapter Nine

 familiar

Someone was there.

Hope tried to wake herself, tried to move. But her body was too heavy to budge, even her pinky finger felt like it was forged from solid lead. She tried to speak but no sound came from her throat. She tried to open her eyes but they remained closed tight.

Jeremy?

Soft touches, like a cool breeze on a humid night, swept over her skin, down her arms, along her cheekbone. She shivered. Warmth trickled through her veins.

Jeremy?

A fingertip found her nipple and traced a slow circle around it. The touch singed her skin, even through the thin fabric of her nightgown. Her breathing echoed loud in her ears, like she was lying in some big, empty space, a tunnel. That same finger dipped down, tracing the cleft between her breasts before finding the other nipple.

She felt her back arching. Her breasts rose into the air, begging for his touch. She fought to find her way out of the darkness but it wouldn't let her go. *Jeremy. I miss you. What have I done?*

Kisses, soft and fleeting tiptoed down her throat. "I'm here, Hope."

Jeremy! Her heart beat a rapid staccato in her chest. *You're here. Please, tell me you'll stay with me.* Eager to touch him, to hold him, she struggled to lift her arms but they wouldn't budge.

"I'm here for now, Hope."

Tell me what to do. How can I fix this?

"Release your heart. Let go of your fear."

She felt him press his lips to hers yet was powerless to return his kiss. His words echoed in her head as his touches played over her body. She felt him pull her nightgown up and heard herself gasp. His fingers traced fiery paths up and down her body yet she lay immobile, like a corpse. Her bones, muscles and nerves refused to follow her command. She felt trapped. Powerless.

Jeremy? Show me.

"I've tried. It's up to you now," his voice hummed through her body like a bolt of electricity. It buzzed in her belly, bouncing around until it rolled into a tight, hot ball.

Smooth waves of warmth rushed out from the ball, like ripples in a pool around a dropped stone. She felt her face flush, felt her chest warm, felt her nipples tighten.

"You are the only woman for me." He kissed her stomach, low, just above the waistband of her panties.

She felt his fingertips as they caught her panties and slowly slid them down over her hips then down her legs.

"Open yourself to me."

I can't. I can't move. I want to.

"Open yourself to me," he repeated. His voice was rich and heavy in her ear. His fingertips dug into her flesh on her thighs as he gently parted them. "I want all of you, Hope. Will you give me all of you? Hold nothing back?"

Jeremy? How? How do I give myself to anyone, most of all a spirit? Old fears bubbled up inside her — giving herself to any man was a recipe for heartbreak. How much more so to a man who couldn't offer her a "normal" life? She heard her breath quicken as he nuzzled her mound then parted her folds with his fingers.

His tongue laved at her slit, drawing the heat from her belly and pulling it lower. It spiraled, whirling round and round, faster, faster, hotter, hotter. He found her clit and teased it with quick thrusts.

The muscles she couldn't control trembled, her legs, her arms, her stomach. Her hips rocked back and forth. Her legs pulled further apart. Her head felt like it was floating in thick soup. Her thoughts bobbed up and down like buoys on waves.

Oh…

"That's the way. Release your heart."

I don't know what that means.

He slowly pressed two fingers into her passage and a sigh of pleasure bubbled around in her chest but refused to find its way out. He hooked them, scraping his knuckles against the sensitive upper wall as he found her clit again with his mouth. Sharp spikes of need shot through her body with each swipe of his tongue and stroke of his fingers.

His words and touches sent hot balls of fire through her body. They pummeled the icy wall encasing her heart, threatening to shatter it.

He quickened the pace. His fingers slid in and out, his tongue danced over her clit. Her body blazed and trembled. She was there, at the cusp of release, her body a tight coil of need, her spirit alighting, free at last of the heavy weight holding it down.

As the first spasm of orgasm gripped her, the ice casing around her heart shattered and she screamed into the empty darkness, "I love you! Come to me. Please. I want you. I...need you. You make me whole."

"That's all you needed to do. I'm here." She felt him withdraw his fingers from her pulsing, gripping pussy, leaving the pleasant tingles and heady warmth of an orgasmic afterglow.

A second later, she blinked open her eyes, disappointed she'd woken. Her heart ached for him. "Oh Jeremy." Hot tears ran down her cheeks as her gaze skittered around the room.

Of course he wasn't there.

It had been a dream. No, more than a dream. That wonderful moment had been real. The indisputable proof was her nudity. But he still couldn't come to her as he had before. She would never see his face, feel his silky curls, lie under his weight after lovemaking.

She stood on shaky legs and went to the window. It was still dark outside. Dark and still and quiet.

A soft rustling behind her caught her attention. Curious, she turned around.

Did she have a mouse infestation?

Another rustle, like the sound of paper being crumpled into a ball sent her hurrying across the room toward the adjoining bathroom.

"Hope."

"Holy shit!" The sight of Jeremy made her heart stop completely. She nearly fell over with fright and surprise and reached forward, swinging her arms in a wide arc, to catch herself from falling. Her hands landed on two very wide, very solid shoulders. "Jeremy?"

He smiled down at her as she stared up into his eyes. Deep blue with flashes of wicked promises.

She shuddered. "You're here? For real?"

"I am."

"But how?" She stared up at his face then pressed her body against his, wishing she could literally melt into his skin. "I've missed you."

"So you said. I missed you too." He wrapped his arms around her in a warm hug and she pressed her ear to his chest. She heard the steady beat of his heart.

"You're really here!" She tipped her head up to look at him. Her arms tightened around his neck. Her fingers tangled in the silky curls at his nape. "What a wonderful surprise. I was so sure I'd never see you again. Can you stay forever?"

"No," he said, sounding regretful. "I'm afraid I can't. I have good news and bad news. Which one do you want to hear first?"

A lump of fear plopped into the pit of her belly. "The bad. Tell me the bad first."

"I can't stay here with you all the time."

"Darn. But you said all the time. What does that mean? Can you stay some of the time? How did this happen? How did you come back? What're the rules?"

He chuckled and toyed with a stray strand of her hair and she smiled into his mischief-filled eyes. "So many questions," he said with one side of his lips curled up into a naughty half-grin.

"Well, you're dead and the CD is broken and you were gone and now you're here and I don't know what it means—" she rambled, excitement taking the place of dread in her tummy and sending a flurry of nervous butterflies flying through her innards.

"Easy, baby. Let's take it one question at a time." He gently extricated himself from her tight grip and led her to the bed. He sat then pulled her onto his lap. "Do you remember what you said a little bit ago?"

"When? Before or after I said, 'Holy shit!'?"

"Before."

"When I was asleep?"

"Yes."

"Huh. Okay." She tried to recall what she'd said but couldn't. She knew she'd had a dream, remembered he was in it, but couldn't remember if she'd said anything.

Maybe it had been something bad?

Something that wouldn't allow him to come back and stay with her forever. "If I said something bad when I was asleep then surely you wouldn't hold me responsible. After all, who has control over what they say when they're dreaming?"

His laughter tickled her insides like merry bubbles. "You didn't say anything bad."

"Whew. That's a relief. I rarely ever remember all the details of my dreams."

"Then let me refresh your memory." He lifted a hand to palm her cheek. "You said you loved me."

She felt the skin under his hand heating. "I said... that?"

"You sure did." He pressed a kiss to her mouth then nibbled the corner of her lip. "You said you wanted me, needed me. I know you meant those words."

"Yeah?" Her eyelids shuttered closed as his hand dropped to her breast. He pinched her nipple and pulled it until it was painfully erect. His tongue and lips continued to perform magical things on her mouth. The man could kiss like no one she'd ever known. His tongue delved into her mouth, stroking, tasting, mating with hers. But the kiss wasn't all tongue. Teeth bit gently at her lower lip. And his lips, damp and soft, slanted over hers, whispering promises that made her tingle from head to toe.

"I wouldn't be here if you hadn't." The hand that had been teasing her nipple slid slowly down her torso until it was at the juncture of her thighs. "I want to make love to you now. But—"

He didn't have to ask twice! Those few touches and kisses had sparked a raging inferno. And his hand sliding down between her legs acted like gasoline, flaring the flame even brighter.

"Yes," she said on a sigh.

His body tight, his cock straining against the front of his trousers, Jeremy scooped her into his arms as he stood. His heart clenched in the steely grip of both profound joy and sorrow, he turned around to lay her on the bed then took a moment to let his gaze wander over her lovely form, each swell and curve. He hoped to burn the images into his memory, so they would be with him always, even when he returned to the gray world without her.

The hunger in her eyes called his gaze to hers. It was held hostage there for several moments until she let her eyelids fall closed, releasing it. "Jeremy," she whispered. The sound slipped through pink-stained, slightly parted lips. Full and sweet. He knew what pleasure they could give, how they had gently encased his cock and stoked the furnace inside to blazing temperatures. The memory of their last night together made his heart hammer out several irregular beats and he had to force himself to resist giving in to the temptation to take rather than give back to her.

"Tonight is for you, my sweet," he promised. "Every minute of it." He knew what she needed, not only her body but what her mind and spirit required as well. It was just a matter of fulfilling those needs. In serving her, he hoped he would receive his reward, her love and trust. But what price would he have to pay?

They had to go now, before he changed his mind. This was what she wanted, it would bring her the affirmation she needed, the faith in herself—and hopefully in him too—that she longed for.

It was no easy task to turn from that beautiful sight, of Hope lying on the bed, her quick breaths and tensed spine thrusting her uncovered breasts high in the air. Pink-tipped nipples stood erect, beckoning his mouth, dry from his hunger.

A short, neat crop of curls at the apex of her thighs hid her sex from his view. Yet, in his mind's eye he saw it as he had the last time they'd been together, wet and open and ready for him. When he inhaled he caught the gentle scent of her natural perfume. Sweet and musky. He longed to taste her.

He strode across the room quickly, hoping to find some clothes for her so they could get going. Instead, as he searched her closet for jeans and a top, maybe a pair of tennis shoes, he found some silk scarves, four of them that he couldn't seem to put down. They'd come in handy later…if… He didn't finish the thought because it hurt too much to consider the possibilities.

The scarves in hand, but no clothes, he returned to the bed and murmured, "I want to tie you up with these, but—"

Her eyelids fluttered open and she looked at his fists, each one gripping two scarves. Her face flushed a sexy shade of magenta. "Okay."

Her eager acquiescence made it doubly hard for him to resist the temptation to stay there and make love to her but the nagging voice of his conscience kept him from caving in.

Later, he reassured himself. He'd only have to wait a little longer. But it would be worth it.

Her deepest wishes, her darkest fantasies were his commands.

"I am your king," he said in his most authoritative voice. "And you will serve my every need, wench."

She squirmed as he said that last word, the corners of her mouth lifting into a sexy smile. "Mmm. My king? Does his highness like what he sees?"

"Very much." He caught her shoulders and pulled until she was sitting. "But before we can think about having some fun with these, we need to do a couple of things."

If he hadn't already been dead, the agony of walking away from a willing and ready Hope would've killed him. "I haven't told you the good news yet."

"You haven't? I could've sworn there was some good news in there somewhere."

"I love you, Hope. No matter what happens tonight, I want you to remember that. Okay?" He waited for her reaction to his words. He could see it was taking a moment for them to sink in.

She blinked once. She blinked twice. Her bottom lip quivered a tiny bit as she stood. "You just said you loved me. Right? Did I hear you say that? Or…or did I hear you wrong?"

He gathered her hands into his and kissed her knuckles. "Yes, you heard me right. I love you very much. Do you want me to repeat it again?"

She gave him a shy smile. "Would you mind?"

"Not a bit." This time, he pulled her closer until her soft body pressed against his. He wrapped his arms around her, dropped his chin onto the top of her head and closed his eyes, relishing the simple joy of just holding her. "Hope Love Hart, I love you." He kissed her coconut-scented hair.

She tipped her head to meet his gaze. "I love you too, Jeremy. More than I've ever loved anyone."

Her confession made him feel warm and soft inside. He felt a dopey smile spreading over his face. "Don't forget what I said. Don't forget I love you. Tonight, of all nights, I need you to remember that."

Her brow furrowed with concern and she gripped his upper arms and shook them. "Hold up! You just told me you love me and I just told you I love you. That's supposed to be The End. We're supposed to live happily ever after, ride off into the sunset, and yadda, yadda, yadda."

He fought back a chuckle. He'd never thought she'd believe in that riding into the sunset stuff, or at least he hadn't thought she'd ever admit it aloud. "We're not quite at that point yet, love. But almost," he said, trying to reassure her. He gently pried her fingers from his arms and stroked hers. "I mean—"

"Almost?" she squeaked. "What do you mean 'almost'?" She shoved at his chest. Not too hard, just hard enough to let him know she meant business. "You don't understand. I don't say those words to anyone but I said them to you. And now you're giving me some vague warnings and telling me we're not ready to call it a night and be happy for the rest of our lives—or...or my life and your afterlife?" She leveled an I-mean-business gaze at him and said, "Give it to me straight. I need to know. What's going to happen? What're you trying to tell me?"

"I'm trying to explain. We're going to go find Timmy now. He's still alive and I know where he is."

Chapter Ten

ℰℭ

"Should we call the police?" Hope asked as she followed Jeremy's directions. Turning left down Main Street and driving into the heart of downtown, she eyed the quiet streets, still deeply shadowed, despite the first spark of daylight tinting the eastern sky a paler shade of blue.

"I'm not sure. They can't do anything about Bergmann."

"What about Timmy?"

"They might help him. Last I saw, he was fine. Scared but okay. The bastard hadn't hurt him. Must've had someone bringing food and water all this whole time. Did you bring your cell phone just in case?"

"Yes." She drove the rest of the way in silence, wondering exactly how this was going to work. If Bergmann was indeed practically invincible, then how would they stop him?

Jeremy instructed her to drive down a bumpy gravel alley, cutting behind a row of old, unkempt Victorian homes on the fringes of town, on the wrong side — quite literally — of the railroad tracks, where the once glorious Victorian ladies had been stripped of their gingerbread trimmings and divided into multiple unit rental properties. Despite the recent warm, wet weather, the backyard had not a single blade of grass, just lots of rutted mud. Several stripped car frames sat on concrete blocks where there should've been a flower garden or a children's play structure. Hardly a garden enthusiast's dream.

"Lovely place," Hope muttered. "Evidently being among the undead doesn't pay too great."

"Considering he can't give a landlord or employer a social security number, I'd say the guy's not doing too bad. This might be the slums, but it's the slum of Plymouth. Hardly Detroit."

"You have a point." She put the car into park and climbed out, stepping into ankle-deep slime. "Ick, if I'd known I'd be trudging through this stuff, I'd have worn boots."

"Sorry, baby. When I visited here in spirit form, I didn't feel the mud."

"Not a problem." She felt her nose wrinkling as the muck seeped into her socks, chilling her ankles. "I didn't wear my very best shoes or socks. Let's go. But before we get up there and all you-know-what breaks loose, you want to fill me in on what to expect?"

"Honey, if I knew, I'd be glad to."

"You have no idea?"

"None."

"Then what're we doing here?"

"Saving that kid."

"I'm calling the police." She took the phone out of her pocket, flipped it open and punched in 911. When the operator answered, Hope gave her the address and told her she had reason to suspect a kidnapped child was being hidden in the basement level apartment. The operator told her to hold then took the details and informed her a car was on the way. The dispatcher told her to wait outside for help.

She flipped the phone closed and nodded to Jeremy. "We're supposed to wait out here. Considering the fact that I don't want to be a hero or zombie slayer or whatever, I think I'll wait out here."

"Good idea." He pulled her to him for a quick embrace and kiss then released her and walked toward the entry at the back of the house.

She caught his hand and gave it a sharp yank. "Where are you going?"

"Inside." He gently peeled her fingers from his wrist, one at a time. "You stay here. It's probably better this way."

"I'm not so sure about that."

"We already discussed this and we don't have time now. The police'll be here in a few minutes. You'll be safe out here, and won't be a suspect. If I'm successful ushering Bergmann back to the spirit world, you'll be left standing in that apartment, your fingerprints all over the place with a kidnapped child. I won't let you walk into that kind of situation."

This time she lunged at him and grabbed his upper arms, one in each hand. And to show him exactly how upset she was about all of this, she gave them both a solid shake. Naturally, her best efforts didn't faze him. "Yeah. But what if something happens to you?"

"I have a strong feeling something's going to happen to me. Bergmann's a very powerful spirit."

"Oh. Is that why he didn't vanish when the CD broke?" she asked. Pieces of the puzzle started fitting together, creating a very frightening image.

"The more evil the spirit, the more power they possess in this world. I'm not sure how I'll get him back to the other side."

That image just became ten times more horrifying. "Will you be hurt? Will you have to go back with him? What'll happen to you?"

"I'm not sure yet."

"I don't like the sound of this at all."

"I know, baby. But we have to do this."

"Would I be selfish if I asked how you'll come back?" she asked, not wanting to voice her real question—if he'd be able to come back. She simply couldn't speak those words.

"Just remember I love you. Forever. You must remember that. It's our only hope."

"Don't do this then. If it means you have to go away...oh, shoot! What am I saying? I'm so confused. This is my fault and now I'm paying the price. And you too."

"Try not to think of it that way." He gave her a final kiss, stroked her lower lip with his thumb and then gently pried her off his body. "I love you."

"I love you too, Jeremy." She watched as he busted open the door with a concrete block. "Wait!"

He turned to face her.

"Will you answer one question before you go in there?"

"Sure, baby."

"Why didn't you go to the light?"

"Because to me you are the light." He blew her a kiss and walked inside.

Every second seemed to last an eternity as she stood outside, watching the door for a sign that Jeremy was okay. It took more willpower than she ever thought she possessed to keep from dashing inside to check.

The police arrived, several cars, a fire truck and ambulance followed behind.

Two officers approached her and listened with curious stares as she explained that she was a psychic and believed the missing child was inside. It was obvious by their expressions that they didn't exactly buy her story but they dutifully agreed to check out the apartment. She left out the part about the guilty party being inhuman, figuring that just might cross the fine line of believability. To ease her guilt, and hoping they'd take more care than normal, she told them she believed the scene inside was extremely dangerous.

They thanked her for her warning then gathered with the other policemen in a huddle. Moments later, guns drawn, they stormed the apartment.

She couldn't remember ever feeling so scared and powerless. She wanted to go inside but knew it wasn't a good idea. She wanted to know what was going on but had no one to tell her. So, she did the wise thing—she paced a three-foot-long path in the mud and waited.

About a lifetime into pacing—yes, it really felt that way—several more police cars rolled up the alley and their passengers raced past her, shouting into their radios.

That didn't bode well.

She resumed pacing, this time doubling her speed, until she plain couldn't stand waiting there another minute and tiptoed up to the apartment's entry.

She heard lots of voices, Jeremy's among them. He was okay! That knowledge made her feel a tad less fearful. Then she heard a child's cry and that made her feel even better. The little boy was alive!

Yet, she was a long way from being ready to do the happy dance. The angry men's voices, no doubt policemen who were struggling to subdue a resistant ghost, told her everything was far from okay yet.

Then, Jeremy's shout—a piercing cry of pain—sent her inching through the doorway.

The action was just inside the door, no more than ten feet from where she stood, clinging to the doorframe. Jeremy and Bergmann were throwing punches at each other, both shaking off policemen like dogs shaking off fleas. One officer shot Jeremy with his taser and he cried out. She saw the agony on his face, in his eyes. For an instant, as an electric charge shot through his body, he seemed to fade a tiny bit, blurred around the edges like an interrupted satellite image.

He wrapped his arms around Bergmann then shouted, "Shoot me now! I'm not releasing him any other way!"

Instantly, she realized what he was doing. She shouted, "Jeremy, I love you too!" She held his pain-stricken gaze for a heartbeat then screamed, "Shoot him with your tasers. All of you!"

The police looked at her, stunned.

"It's the only way to send them back."

One policeman shot Jeremy in the shoulder but the charge wasn't enough. Again, the two ghosts faded, but only for an instant.

"More. They need more electricity."

"That'll kill them, lady," one policeman said. "They should already be flat on their backs as it is. We've shot them twice now."

"They're already dead. Just shoot them."

"Shoot me," Jeremy demanded, struggling to hold Bergmann, who was doing his best to break free of Jeremy's hold before he was sent to hell. "Do it now!"

A couple of policemen looked at each other. Hope lunged forward, snatched a taser from one of them and screamed as she aimed it at Jeremy's shoulder and pulled the trigger.

The charge from her shot, combined with the two from earlier charges made them flicker from view for several seconds and then return.

"Another one," she cried out.

A policeman took aim and fired. The probes clung to Jeremy's shirtsleeve, inches below where the probes from her shot still dangled, sending periodic jolts of electricity through his body.

The first charge from that final shot made both men disappear completely.

The officers waited, their guns lifted, ready.

Hope heard their heavy breathing as she stared at the spot where the two ghosts had been standing.

Neither reappeared.

"I think they're gone," she whispered.

The policemen slowly, one by one, lowered their guns and looked at Hope for answers to the questions none of them spoke.

Another officer escorted the wide-eyed little boy from somewhere beyond the living room, through the space filled with his bewildered coworkers and past Hope out the door.

The little boy raised fear-filled eyes to Hope as he passed and she gave him a reassuring smile. "You'll go home to your mommy and daddy now. You're safe."

The little boy didn't speak as he walked out the door.

Hope followed him outside, suddenly not so concerned about the cold muck sucking her feet. She sat on the hood of her car and waited for the inevitable.

The questioning took over an hour. By then, daylight had shoved the remaining indigo out of its way, filling the sky with clear, spring royal blue. She had no idea what they'd write in their reports. None of them seemed to like the explanation she'd given them but she couldn't help that. It was the truth.

She went home, exhausted, her eyes bleary and burning. Her heart heavy. Her insides feeling empty. She didn't do her normal routine—check email, check phone messages. Instead she went to her room and dropped into her warm bed. She could still catch his scent on her pillow. She hugged it tight to her chest and closed her eyes.

Just like the night before, he came to her in her dreams, kissed away her tears and whispered, "I'll be back tomorrow night to finish what I started this morning. And I'll return every night after that. Your love will bridge our worlds, but only after the sun sets."

"That's fine with me. Just tell me I won't have to electrocute you every morning to send you back because I don't have the stomach to do that again."

"I have another way…" He lifted a hand, displaying a CD with a plain black label. "This one won't bring me to you but it'll send me back. And it's a great deal more humane than the charges from a half-dozen taser guns. That hurt like hell."

"Much worse than with the CD?"

"A little," he admitted with a guilty shrug.

"I knew you were lying. Why'd you lie?" she asked, not angry this time, just curious.

"I didn't want you to feel guilty. It's not like I can't handle it. I can. I just want you to be happy, Hope."

"That I am. And even if I can't have you all day, I don't care. The nights are ours, right? Every night?"

"Yes, every night," he whispered, his voice full of wicked promise.

She wanted to touch him. She reached out. Her arm sliced right through him. She stared at it then up at his face. "You know I never wanted to get married. This'll be better than marriage. You'll be like my husband in all the ways that count. Right?"

"Yes, baby. In all ways that matter to you." He leaned down, kissed the top of her head and set the CD on the bed. "I'll even take care of the garbage and toilet."

"Thank you." She glanced down at the CD then up again at his face, the face she adored, the face she dreamed about, the face she would cherish every day for the rest of her life.

"No biggie. It's only a toilet. I can handle it." He smiled. His grape-juice-hued eyes sparkled.

She giggled. "No. Thank you for obliterating my fear of needing someone, relying on them. I hadn't realized how much power I'd let that fear have over me. For that, I owe you an eternity of fantasies."

"And I love you too."

And so, Hope Love Hart spent every night with Jeremy living out their fantasies, and he continued to help her with her work, until it was her turn to cross the barrier between their worlds and join him for eternity.

The End

Enjoy this excerpt from
Wet and Wilde
© Copyright Tawny Taylor, 2004

Another girl's night — in hell

If there was one thing Jane Wilde knew it was that she'd trade her left boob to avoid another pathetic Saturday night at Diana's, swapping complaints about the slim pickin's in the man department. In fact, she'd give up both boobs. Her stiff neck and shoulder muscles would thank her.

She sure didn't want to be reminded of how pitiful her love life was at the moment.

Bucket of popcorn the size of a small bathtub in one hand, a glass of diet cola, since she was on a diet, in the other, she took her prescribed seat on the couch. "Please tell me we aren't watching another vampire flick. I'm vamped out. And if I didn't know better," she paused to stab at her best friend and confidante, Diana, with a finger, "I'd swear your teeth have grown at least a quarter inch."

"Nope. No vamps today." Diana gave Jane a toothy grin and scooped up a handful of popcorn, leaving half of it trailing over Jane's lap. "It's mermaids! Splash."

"Oh God, spare me." Jane slid deeper into the super-plush cushions of Diana's sky-blue couch.

"It has Cher in it. How could it be that bad?" Carmen, Jane's other best friend, asked as she rounded the corner from the kitchen, her expression chock-full of wide-eyed hope. "Have you seen it?"

"It's not that movie." Jane fought back the urge to roll her eyes skyward. "Although I wouldn't want to see that one, either. This is the movie with that blonde — what's her name? — walking naked around New York. It's older than I am, and even lamer. The only good thing about it is Tom Hanks. Couldn't you find something better?" She dumped half her cola down her throat, about ready to hit the harder stuff. If this night was going to be salvaged, she'd need something with a lot more kick, like tequila. "Why can't we watch a movie that has nothing to do with mythological creatures, whether they live in dungeons or the sea?"

"Because those creatures are mysterious—sexy!" Diana waggled her eyebrows, her eyes the size of silver dollars, and punched her. "Have you ever considered the possibilities?"

"Possibilities?" Jane shook her head, ignoring Diana's jab to her shoulder. "Not since I quit believing in the Easter Bunny."

Diana gave her another nudge. "Scoot over and quit being such a grouch."

Jane shot Diana an intentionally exaggerated look of admonishment and complied, giving her just enough room for her skinny ass to fit between the couch arm and Jane's admittedly wider one. "Next week, I choose."

Diana clucked her tongue and shook her head. "You know the rules, the hostess picks the movie. And next week it's Carmen's turn."

Carmen nodded her head.

This time Jane didn't bother stopping her eyes from rolling. "And Carmen calls you from the video store every time."

"Well, if you answered your phone occasionally," Carmen piped in, sounding a touch defensive, "I'd call you, too."

"You both know why I don't. That man won't stop calling me, divorce or not. He's such a control freak."

"Maybe it's time to change your number," Diana offered.

Jane shot up from the couch. Yep, it was definitely time for that drink. She drained her glass on her way to the kitchen, leaving the other two women to their discussion about next week's torture. No doubt it would be some sort of monster-mermaid-superman flick. If only she had something better to do!

She stooped down, rummaging through Diana's eternally well-stocked refrigerator. The woman kept enough food in there for an army, and ate a truckload at every meal.

Jane hated her…kinda.

"Where're the wine coolers?" she shouted.

"Carmen's polishing off the last one," Diana answered. "You want me to go to the store for more?"

Drag! No alcohol? A movie released before she had filled out her first bra, and nothing to sweeten the deal. Could this night be any worse? "No, that's okay." She refilled her glass with diet cola and headed back to the living room.

Both ladies smiled at her. Smiled like they'd just signed a pact with the devil. Like they'd just enlisted her in the army. Like they'd just promised her life in return for...something.

Uh oh. "What?"

"We have an idea," Diana stood and reached for Jane's arm.

"Yeah, a really great idea." Carmen reached for the other arm.

Sandwiched between two conniving women? That was one place she didn't want to be. She tugged but quickly realized they weren't going to let her go. "What kind of idea?" She really didn't want to know.

Carmen giggled. "Since your birthday's coming up—"

"It was last month," Jane interrupted.

"Even better!" Diana released her arm and gave her shoulders a sound shove, knocking her backward onto the couch. "Sit. Shut up. And listen. This is for your own good."

Diana could sure be one bossy bitch! It almost pissed Jane off the way Diana was literally pushing her around. She prepared to deliver a choice word or two, but reminded herself of the past six months.

Yep, after holding Jane up for six months, the least her well-meaning friend had earned was a license to shove.

Jane glanced at Carmen, and Carmen gave her a reassuring smile.

"Okay," she said on a sigh. "What's this great idea?"

"For your birthday, we'd like to give you a wish. A makeover. New clothes, new attitude on life. What do you say?"

"New attitude? What's wrong with the one I have?" She wasn't sure she liked what their grand scheme implied. Was she that pitiable? Were her clothes that outdated?

"Nothing, really." Carmen sat on the coffee table. "But we just thought you could use—" She shrugged. "Something to make you feel better, now that— Well, you know."

Did they have to keep mentioning that? "I'm fine—outside of my phone ringing off the damn hook, and the two people I call my best friends bull-dogging me into something I don't want to do."

Diana sat on the table and shoved Carmen aside. "You're making her feel worse. Let me try." Diana sighed. "Listen, sweetie. Everyone who goes through a change in life—good or bad—has to adjust. That goes for you, too. And to ease that adjustment, it's good to do something positive, for yourself."

"Like get surgery to make myself look like Pamela Anderson?" Jane asked, fighting a smile.

"Sure!" Carmen nodded her head.

"Seriously." Diana gave Jane a swift smack on the thigh— ouch! "Get with the program here. Isn't there anything you have wanted to do for yourself? Something that's been nagging at you for a long, long time?"

"I've wanted to get plastic surgery," Carmen interjected. "I'd love to look like Pamela—at least from the neck to about here." She motioned just below her very flat boobs.

Diana smiled. "Okay, sweetie." She gave Carmen's shoulder a squeeze. "We'll get you that surgery when your birthday comes."

Carmen grinned, her pink-tinged face getting even redder, clashing with her carrot-hued hair. "You will! Gosh, that's mighty nice of you!"

Jane watched Carmen, all aglow, and thought about the possibilities. Okay, the idea of having a wish was kind of cool. Something for herself? Something that would make her feel better? Then, the idea struck her. "I've always wanted to learn how to swim."

In an instant, memories of sultry days on the beach with her brothers and sisters came to mind. Days when they enjoyed the fresh coolness of the sea while she sat frozen by fear at the shore, willing herself to take a leap into that terrifying, roiling mass. She couldn't remember exactly when that fear had surfaced, vaguely recalled nearly drowning as a young child. But she sure would like to shake it now.

Diana's smile couldn't get any bigger than it was, and dread slipped down Jane's spine.

"Perfect," Diana said, slapping her hands on her thighs. "I know the perfect person to teach you, too. I mean I don't know him personally, but I know of him. He's a world-class swimmer and to-die-for to boot."

"No way." Jane shot to her feet. She was at least twenty pounds overweight, and the Slim Fast shakes weren't doing a bit of good. God, she looked terrible in a swimsuit! Jiggly thighs, an ass that made J-Lo's look tiny…

Diana stopped her before she was completely on her feet and knocked her back on her ass. "You're not backing out. Not a chance. I'm calling. I'm scheduling your class. And I'm taking you, and there isn't a damn thing you can do about it."

Except not show up.

"And don't think you can hide from me." Diana finished, as if she could read Jane's mind. "I will find you, and you will go. If it makes you feel any better, I'll take the class with you."

"Great. So, when I drown, I can take you down with me." Jane crossed her arms over her chest. Granted, Diana had been a lifesaver—literally—recently, but that didn't give her the right to force her to do anything. Last time Jane checked she was over eighteen—by a few years.

Besides, the idea of standing mostly unclothed next to emaciated Diana was enough to make her vomit.

About the Author

❧

Nothing exciting happens in Tawny Taylor's life, unless you count giving the cat a flea dip—a cat can make some fascinating sounds when immersed chin-deep in insecticide—or chasing after a houseful of upchucking kids during flu season. She doesn't travel the world or employ a staff of personal servants. She's not even built like a runway model. She's just your run-of-the-mill, pleasantly plump Detroit suburban mom and wife.

That's why she writes, for the sheer joy of it. She doesn't need to escape, mind you. Despite being run-of-the-mill, her life is wonderful. She just likes to add some...zip.

Her heroines might resemble herself, or her next door neighbor (sorry Sue) but they are sure to be memorable (she hopes!). And her heroes—inspired by movie stars, her favorite television actors or her husband—are fully capable of delivering one hot happily-ever-after after another. Combined, the characters and plots she weaves bring countless hours of enjoyment to Tawny...and she hopes to readers too!

In the end, that's all the matters to Tawny, bringing a little bit of zip to someone else's life.

Tawny welcomes mail from readers. You can write to her c/o Ellora's Cave Publishing at 1056 Home Avenue, Akron OH 44310-3502.

Why an electronic book?

We live in the Information Age—an exciting time in the history of human civilization in which technology rules supreme and continues to progress in leaps and bounds every minute of every hour of every day. For a multitude of reasons, more and more avid literary fans are opting to purchase e-books instead of paperbacks. The question to those not yet initiated to the world of electronic reading is simply: *why?*

1. *Price.* An electronic title at Ellora's Cave Publishing and Cerridwen Press runs anywhere from 40-75% less than the cover price of the <u>exact same title</u> in paperback format. Why? Cold mathematics. It is less expensive to publish an e-book than it is to publish a paperback, so the savings are passed along to the consumer.

2. *Space.* Running out of room to house your paperback books? That is one worry you will never have with electronic novels. For a low one-time cost, you can purchase a handheld computer designed specifically for e-reading purposes. Many e-readers are larger than the average handheld, giving you plenty of screen room. Better yet, hundreds of titles can be stored within your new library—a single microchip. (Please note that Ellora's Cave and Cerridwen Press does not endorse any specific brands. You can check our website at www.ellorascave.com or

www.cerridwenpress.com for customer recommendations we make available to new consumers.)

3. *Mobility.* Because your new library now consists of only a microchip, your entire cache of books can be taken with you wherever you go.

4. *Personal preferences are accounted for.* Are the words you are currently reading too small? Too large? Too...**ANNOYING**? Paperback books cannot be modified according to personal preferences, but e-books can.

5. *Instant gratification.* Is it the middle of the night and all the bookstores are closed? Are you tired of waiting days—sometimes weeks—for online and offline bookstores to ship the novels you bought? Ellora's Cave Publishing sells instantaneous downloads 24 hours a day, 7 days a week, 365 days a year. Our e-book delivery system is 100% automated, meaning your order is filled as soon as you pay for it.

Those are a few of the top reasons why electronic novels are displacing paperbacks for many an avid reader. As always, Ellora's Cave and Cerridwen Press welcomes your questions and comments. We invite you to email us at service@ellorascave.com, service@cerridwenpress.com or write to us directly at: 1056 Home Ave. Akron OH 44310-3502.

MAKE EACH DAY MORE EXCITING WITH OUR

ELLORA'S CAVEMEN Calendar

www.EllorasCave.com